I0736022

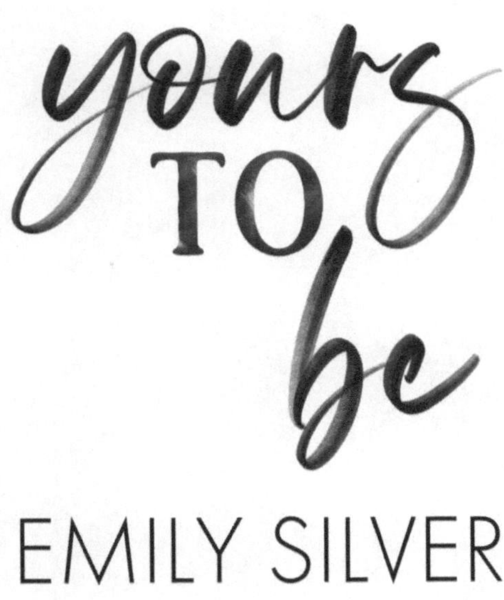

EMILY SILVER

TRAVELIN' HOOSIER BOOKS

Copyright © 2023 by Emily Silver

All rights reserved.

No part of this book may be reproduced in any form or by any electronic or mechanical means, including information storage and retrieval systems, without written permission from the author, except for the use of brief quotations in a book review.

Cover Design by Ya'll That Graphic

Editing by Happily Editing Anns

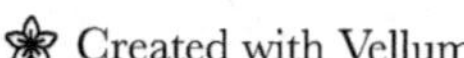 Created with Vellum

To everyone with a dick of an ex
This one's for you

Author's Note

Dear Reader,

Pierce here. You might recognize me from Royal Relations. Fun fact you might not have known – The Winchester Family are Sean and mine's cousins. Sean dropped into Dixon in Royal Reckoning (where you met Gemma), but now we're coming to town!

You can read Royal Reckoning if you want—

Sean: Pierce!

Oops. Gotta run.

See you in Dixon!
Pierce

Chapter One

LAYLA

Clack. Clack. Clack.

Snip. Pin. Repeat.

The whir of the sewing machine is the only sound echoing around my empty studio.

Bits of fabric are strewn everywhere. White lace and silk are pinned to the mannequin across the room, holding up the bodice of the wedding dress I'm currently working on.

The exquisite fabric is like butter as I push it through the machine, watching the skirt come together.

This is the first wedding dress I've ever created.

Pushing back the wispy blonde hairs that have escaped my bun, I snip the threads and inspect the hem of the skirt. Pearls and lace shimmer against the silk.

When this is done, it's going to be one of the most beautiful things I've ever made. My smile is bright as the door creaks open and my assistant pops her head in.

"Layla. Sorry to interrupt, but a customer was hoping to meet you. She loves the Summer Bouquet shirt, and wants to meet the designer."

"Be right out."

I set the skirt down with care. The last thing I need is for anything to damage it this close to the wedding.

My sister loves me and all, but if her wedding dress gets ruined, I don't know if I'll ever hear the end of it.

"Where is she?" I ask Erica, my eyes scanning the crowded store.

She points to the back corner. "On the platform."

A woman with red, flowing hair is spinning, hands running all over the material of my summer statement piece.

"Hi there. You wanted to see me?" I ask, trying not to startle her.

"I asked the sales associate if I could meet the designer. I don't think I've ever seen anything so fabulous in my life."

A blush creeps across my cheeks at her words. I don't know if I'll ever tire of hearing how much someone loves my work.

"That was me."

"Shut up! You designed this?" The customer standing in front of the three-way mirror turns to face me. "How are you not on *Project Runway* or something? I feel like a rock star in this."

I smile at her, taking in my latest completed creation. The off-the-shoulder top has a bursting floral print and wide bell sleeves that split open before tying at the bottom. It needs little else other than a simple skirt to go with it. It's a statement all on its own.

"I'm happy creating my clothes here."

She pulls her phone out of her back pocket, snapping some photos. "I have to tell everyone I know about this place. It's a hidden gem."

"Are you from around here?" I ask.

She shakes her head. "My boyfriend is in town hiking

this week. I came along, but it's not really my thing. I'm having a spa weekend over at the ranch outside of town."

Now it makes sense how she found me. Gemma surely must have sent her my way. My shop is tucked away off the main town square. It's one of the smaller storefronts in town, but all I could afford when I opened.

"Are you enjoying your stay over there?"

She nods, snapping her gum. "Totally. It's like one big Instagram photo op."

"As long as you're enjoying it." I try not to laugh. "Is there anything else I can help you find?"

"What else have you designed in here? I need one of everything."

"The summer collection is dwindling, but I do have a few more of the lingerie sets that might interest you."

Her mouth drops open in awe. "You design lingerie? I have to see it."

The excitement coming off her in waves makes me just as excited. Walking over to the small selection in the corner of the store, I pull out my favorite set for her.

The black fabric is sheer, strung through with bursts of gold silk thread. It's like the night sky exploding over the cups of the bra. Gold peeks out of the lining, giving a hint if you wear a low-cut top as to what's underneath.

It's stunning. The hipster thong that matches is just as beautiful.

"Okay, do you sell online? Because I need to get this and everything else you design."

"I'll get you a card. I'm Layla."

She takes my extended hand in a firm handshake. "Bri Edwards."

"Nice to meet you. I'll let you finish looking around, and if you need anything else, let me know."

"Thanks, Layla."

The shop is busy. For a beautiful summer day, I'd expect it to be quieter. In the shadow of the Tetons, our town brings in nature enthusiasts, and today is the perfect outdoor day.

I like it that way because it lets me sew. My favorite place to be in the world is behind my sewing machine in my tiny studio, creating pieces to help women like Bri feel beautiful.

The bells above the door chime as someone new walks into the store. Someone that immediately sets me on edge.

"Layla, dear." Mrs. Bush walks into the store, a purpose to her stride.

I steel my face. The last thing I want to deal with today is Mrs. Bush, the mayor's secretary.

A.k.a. my ex-husband's secretary.

"How are you?"

"Tryin' to beat this heat. Too damn hot this summer." She shakes her head, her short curls bouncing back and forth.

"Can I get you something to drink?"

She waves me off. "I'm fine. Do you have a few minutes to chat?"

"I'm free. What do you need?"

An uneasy feeling settles in my stomach.

Mrs. Bush hands over a sheet of paper. *Application denied* is stamped in big red letters on the top of the page.

"The larger space is unavailable."

"Since when?" I try to keep my voice down, but it's hard. "As of this morning, it's still sitting empty."

I can see it every day from my studio apartment above my shop. The "for lease" sign hasn't moved in months.

"Since we got the paperwork this morning." Her bejeweled glasses make her look friendlier than her posture lets on. For an older woman who loves nothing more than gossiping with the rest of the old biddies in town, she's not the nicest of people.

I chalk that up to her being my third grade teacher. I don't know how this woman ever taught children. She's the most unpleasant person in town. She was harsh even back then. I don't think she ever liked me. I had a penchant for getting into trouble because my mind was always wandering. Playing with cut-out paper dolls instead of listening in class.

To this day, I still think she doesn't like me.

"That building has been gathering dust for years since Old Man Reynolds closed the general store."

She shrugs, her glasses sliding down her nose. "I'm not allowed to disclose any details of the new deal. The mayor made sure of it."

"I'll bet he did," I grumble.

"Dear, that's a big space. Do you even have the money for the lease?"

Her coddling tone nearly sends me over the edge. "Of course I do. Look around,"—I wave my hand around the store—"business has never been better."

And thank God the store is crowded today. I can't imagine what her face would look like if it were empty.

"Nevertheless, word is a new company is setting up shop in town."

"What company?" I stare her dead in the eye.

Nice tone be damned.

"That's not for you to worry about."

"It is if you're giving them the building that I'm trying to lease."

She purses her lips at me. "Not trying. Sorry, Layla, but that's the final word."

"And nothing I say will change your mind?"

"You can try talking to the mayor, but I doubt it."

Sticking her nose in the air, she gives my store a once-over, like it's one of the most offensive places she's ever stepped foot in.

"Have a nice day, Layla." With a wave, she's out of the store.

"Fuck." I look at the paper in my hand.

All my hard work over the last few months down the drain by one company moving into town. Supposedly.

"What was that about?" Erica, my shop assistant, pops up by my shoulder.

"We didn't get the Reynolds building."

"You're kidding."

I hand over the piece of paper. "She just dropped it off. Says there's a new company coming into town."

"What company? We would've heard about it."

Erica is outraged on my behalf, fuming next to me.

Pinstripes & Push-Ups is everything I've spent my adult career working toward. While I buy a lot of pieces from designers, I work night and day to bring my own fashion to life.

Dresses, tops, lingerie. I want people to come into my shop and leave feeling better about themselves.

P&P is now bursting at the seams. With trying to grow my online business, staying within these four walls is proving a lot harder than I thought.

If I want to grow, I need more space.

The building on Main Street, right in the heart of Dixon, would be the perfect place to expand. Gorgeous brick walls with old-fashioned overhead lighting. It's everything I've wanted in a new store.

Except my ex-husband has denied the application.

Fucking ex-husbands.

He doesn't know who he's messed with.

Chapter Two

SIMON

"**Y**ou're such a wanker."

"You just can't take being a sore loser."

Taking a swig of my water, I squirt a stream of it at Pierce, one of my oldest friends. "I wouldn't be a sore loser if you didn't cheat."

"Who says I'm cheating?"

"Me." I wipe the sweat from my brow. "You were offside and you know it!"

He gives me a cocky grin. "If the ref didn't call it, it wasn't cheating."

This is the problem with playing footie with friends—Liam wasn't paying attention because his new girl was here watching us play.

"We need new refs," I grumble, collapsing on the bench.

"Or maybe you just need to play better."

I flip him off, grabbing the neck of my shirt and pulling it off. With the heat of the London day now gone, I grab a hoodie and pull it over. The rest of the team has long since left the field.

"Beer?" Pierce hands me an ice-cold bottle.

Twisting off the cap, I clink my beer with his. "Cheers, you lousy cheat."

"Ahh, Simon. You'll learn eventually you can never beat me."

"Careful, or I'm going to send you with newbies to America."

"You wouldn't dare."

"My company. I can send whoever I please." This time, it's me with the smug grin.

"You'd really do that to poor Charlotte?"

"She'd say it's your own fault."

Pierce laughs, a dopey look coming over his face. "You're right. She would."

These days, the only time I see Pierce is at our weekly football match. With two kids now and a princess for a wife, all his spare time is spent with his family.

Not that I can blame him. I've had my fair share of girlfriends these last few years, but none of them want to compete with the job.

And none of them can. Work comes first.

"You still planning on coming over to discuss logistics?" Pierce leans back on his elbows, sipping on his beer.

"If you need me to." I eye him over my own drink. The lights on the field are bright as the city noise gets quieter. "Nervous about taking the family overseas for the first time?"

"Not me. Charlotte is."

"Don't you go blaming me." A sweet voice cuts through the open field.

"What are you doing here, love?" Pierce jumps to his feet, finding his wife. She looks more laid-back than I've seen her lately. With her dark brown hair pulled back into a low ponytail, she's wearing a jumper and joggers.

"Thought I'd come to see you lads play." She walks over to me. "I see he's still cheating." Her laughter rings out bright.

"See! Even your wife thinks so!" I point a finger at him, before dropping a quick peck on Charlotte's cheek. "Hi, Charlotte."

"Et tu, Charlotte?" Pierce acts wounded, but his laughter gives him away.

"Oh, shove off, you. You know you were offside and Liam wasn't paying attention. Who's the new girl?" Charlotte drops down onto the bench next to me.

"We haven't met her yet," I tell her.

"Something about us being huge knobs and him not wanting her to meet us."

Charlotte eyes her husband, then grabs his beer and takes a sip. "Can't imagine why he'd say that."

"Wow. There is no love lost tonight," Pierce tells us. "I'm a perfect gentleman."

"Sure you are."

"Is that why you don't have a girlfriend?" Pierce moves over to Charlotte, resting between her legs.

"Hey, you know my job takes up all my time right now."

"Do we know anyone we could set him up with?" Charlotte asks Pierce, completely ignoring me.

"I can see if Ruby has any friends from school. No one at the foundation?"

Charlotte gives him a thoughtful look. "None that are single."

"Perhaps your gran knows someone. Maybe an older woman is just what he needs," Pierce snickers.

"Oy! You two done yet?" I shake my head, swallowing the last of my beer. "And here to think I get enough grief about my dating life from my mum."

"Poor Simon."

"What Pierce means,"—Charlotte smacks him on the shoulder—"is we just want to make sure you're happy."

"I am happy."

"Are you though? You seem sad. Ever since Lily dumped you," Charlotte points out.

"We mutually called things off."

"Did you though?" Pierce asks.

"Since when did tonight become all about my love life?"

It's been a long time since I've thought of Lily. We dated for a few weeks last year, but called it quits early on. The chemistry just wasn't there.

It seems that all my friends are getting married or partnering off these days. It hasn't bothered me one bit.

Until they point it out like this.

"How about we go back to talking about the plan for when we head to Dixon?" I don't want any attention on me.

"I thought that was all planned out," Charlotte replies. "Did anything new come up to change the plans?"

I clock their security officers. Pierce and Charlotte have their own security team, but when they travel—not on formal royal duties—my company steps in for security at their own cost.

With a trip to the states for a family wedding—a cousin of Sean and Pierce's—we've been on high alert. Travel details have been under lock and key, with no information being disclosed to the press.

"No. Pierce here said you wanted to talk more about it."

Charlotte drops a kiss on his forehead.

To think that all those years ago Pierce was as single as I am. And now he's married to the princess.

"My sweet husband is more worried than I am." She turns a warm smile on me. "I trust you have everything figured out."

"Glad someone trusts me," I mumble.

"It's the first time traveling with two kids. You've met Jane. Never met a stranger."

"Guess she takes after her mum," I tell Pierce.

"I'll make sure Pierce isn't worried."

"I'm heading out next week to make sure everything is in place out there." Standing, I clap Pierce on the shoulder.

"Make sure not to ruffle Gramps's feathers."

"I'm not a feather ruffler."

"Sure you're not." Pierce laughs.

"No, that's your job." He jumps up, looking like he's ready for a fight, as much as two friends can. "Listen, I'll let you two get going."

"We're not worried," Charlotte whispers as she leans up to hug me.

I smile down at her. Her face is makeup-free and happy. "I know. I'll send along the last of the briefs to make sure Pierce knows that too."

The two of them leave, hand in hand.

It's never bothered me before that I don't have anyone in my life. I didn't exactly have the best role model for love growing up.

Maybe I should let them set me up. Not that it's worked in the past.

I'm fine with life how it is. I don't need anyone to complete it.

Work comes first.

And until I meet someone, my eyes are set on Dixon. Everything else can wait.

Chapter Three

"Did you pull the permit requests?" I ask my assistant over Bluetooth. "I have to talk with Brad later this week about the open building."

"You're still going to try and get it?" Erica asks, shuffling papers around on her end.

"I'm not going to let that old bat Mrs. Bush walk all over me."

Erica snorts over the phone. "It'd be pretty hard to do since she's about five inches shorter than you and weighs ninety pounds soaking wet."

"It's the disdain that kills me. God forbid a woman sell lingerie."

"Do you think it's the selling or the people buying it that sets her on edge?"

I turn onto the road leading up to the ranch. "Both. Clearly she's never owned lingerie in her life."

Erica snickers on the other end of the line. "Listen, I'll get a meeting set up with Brad. You don't worry about him—"

"My ex-husband? Of course I'm going to worry about it. Not like he'll give me anything…"

Of all the people to become mayor of our small town, it had to be my ex-husband. He wanted nothing to do with politics when we started dating in college, but now? Now it's his life's dream to become the next governor of our humble state.

And I'll be damned if I let him and that old bat use me as a stepping stone to get there.

"Take care of the dress and I'll take care of this."

I blow out a breath as I pull into an empty spot in front of the ranch. "I don't know what I'd do without you, Erica."

"Let's hope you never have to find out."

She ends the call.

The ranch is blissfully empty. In just a few days, the entire ranch is going to shut down for Gemma and Blake's wedding. With so many family members coming—not just from out of state, but out of country too—they wanted to make it a month-long celebration.

Stepping out of my car, my eye catches on a man dressed in all black. Slinking around the edge of the fence around the barn, he sticks out like a sore thumb.

It's almost eighty degrees today and he's in a suit. I watch as he looks around before going inside.

It isn't someone I recognize.

Oh fuck. He's probably paparazzi sent here to take pictures of the royals. I can't imagine what a photo would go for of them on vacation here.

Slamming my car door, I stalk off toward the barn. There's no way I'm going to let some scum of the earth plant hidden cameras and ruin my sister's wedding.

Fuck no.

Stalking off toward the barn, anger floods my veins. It's

one of the downsides of having family members who are married to royals. They never get any privacy.

The few times I've visited them in London, press is everywhere. It's a shame they can't go about their day in peace.

The barn door is open and I sneak inside.

The mystery man is taking photos of every angle of the barn's interior on his phone. No long-range lens for this guy. Maybe he's planning where to plant cameras for any photo op he can get.

Yet, for a photographer scraping by on photos of famous people, he's different than I expected him to be.

My eyes drink him in. I have no clue who this guy is. In dark shades, he's dressed head to toe in black. A suit no less. The photographers I remember seeing in London were a lot more casual than this.

Old Man River whinnies as I walk past the horse stalls, drawing the visitor's attention to my presence.

"Thanks for nothing." I give him a quick pet before closing the distance between myself and the unwanted guest. "Can I ask what you're doing here?"

"What does it look like I'm doing?"

"Oh good. Paparazzi with attitude."

"Actually,"—he clears his throat—"it's paparazzo. Paparazzi is plural."

If I wasn't so annoyed by this man, I'd be swooning at that deep, British accent of his. Whoever tipped him off got their schedules wrong. Our family from across the pond isn't set to arrive for another few days.

"It doesn't matter. You're not allowed to be here."

"Actually, I am."

"Ugh. Fucking paparazzi."

"Paparazzo."

I roll my eyes. "Do you get off on correcting people you're stalking?"

"I'm sorry, what? Who says I'm stalking anyone?"

I give this man a thorough once-over. Dark sunglasses hide his eyes. Scruff lines his jaw. Freckles dot his face. His light-brown hair is perfectly styled.

The read I'm getting on his face? He's giving me attitude.

The balls on this guy.

"You're trespassing on private property. You have no right to be here."

"I was told this was where I need to be."

The man in question tries to step around me, but I throw out a hand, stopping him. "I don't know who you work for, but you're not getting any pictures of my family."

God, these people really have no limits on what they'll do to grab a photo.

"Wait, you think I'm a paparazzo?" He looks horrified at my accusation.

"It's pretty obvious." I cross my arms. If this guy is going to give me attitude, I can give it back in spades.

"Love, I'm the furthest thing from paparazzi."

I ignore the way he said *love*. How very British of him it is.

"Why should I believe you?"

He pulls a business card from his jacket pocket and hands it over. "Simon Belvy. Private security for the Davies family."

"What?" I take the proffered card from his hand. There it is, written on an all-black business card. Belvy Security.

Shit.

"You're hired security?"

A smirk plays at the corner of his mouth. "Last I checked."

Shit. Shit. Shit. Shit.

"I'm assuming you're related to the bride in some way?" Simon pulls off his sunglasses and—oh Lord. Forest-green eyes assess me in a quick sweep. I don't think I've seen a prettier set of eyes on a man before. Except they are no doubt making a snap decision about me the same way I did about him.

I feel his gaze everywhere.

"I'm the maid of honor."

He smiles at me and it does funny things to my insides.

"I should have guessed."

"What, because I'm protective of her?"

Simon moves in closer to me. "Not just her, but Pierce and Sean too."

I tuck his card in the back pocket of my jeans. "I guess I can believe you since you know my cousins by name."

"Unless I'm playing the long con…" He winks at me.

"Cute." I roll my eyes at him.

"Listen…" he trails off. "Sorry, love, I didn't catch your name."

"Layla." It's clipped. I don't know why I don't want this man to know my name. Although, if he's done any kind of digging into the family, he knows exactly who I am.

"Layla, I'm the man making sure no paparazzi get in here to ruin your sister's big event."

"So you're not hiding cameras in here?" I become very interested in the dirt under my shoes. God, way to make a great first impression, Layla.

Simon uses a knuckle to lift my gaze to meet his. Those green eyes of his show a hint of playfulness.

"The only cameras that will be in here are ones I add for additional security. No one is getting by me."

This close, he smells like tea and lemon. It sends shudders through my body.

Calm down, Layla.

You just accused the man of ruining your sister's wedding, and now you're reacting to him?

Get a grip.

"I guess I should let you get back to it then."

"I'd hate to have to tell everyone that my mission was interrupted by a sexy blonde."

"Does that line ever work on anyone?"

I hope the slight tremble in my voice doesn't show how much the line worked on me.

What woman isn't a sucker for a man with an accent?

"Not a line. I guess I'll be seeing you around then, Layla."

"I guess so, Simon."

Simon slips out of the barn like a thief in the night. I'm left standing here wondering what in the ever-loving hell just happened.

First I accuse him of being a paparazzi—sorry, paparazzo—and now I'm turned on by the sexy Brit that's here for the wedding.

"Layla? What are you doing out here?" Gemma's voice distracts me from my wayward thoughts. "I saw your car out front and came looking."

"Just came to say hi to the horses."

Gemma looks at me like I've lost my mind. And today? I might very well have.

"That's it?"

"No." Walking over to her, I link my arm with hers. "I had a few adjustments I needed to make on your dress and wanted you to give it another try on for me."

"Really?" Her brown eyes are sparkling. "I can't wait to

see. I've got a few minutes before the head of security comes to meet with me for the wedding."

"Security?" I ask. Pretty sure I already bumped into him.

"Didn't I tell you? Charlotte and Ellie hired private security for the month to make sure the wedding goes off without a hitch."

"I'm sure you mentioned it at some point."

If only I had gotten here five minutes later, I might not have made a complete ass of myself in front of one of the sexiest men I remember seeing in a long time.

But given that he's been hired by family, that means he'll be here until the wedding next month.

And I wouldn't mind getting to see a lot more of him between now and then.

Chapter Four

LAYLA

"Aunt Layla!" Willow comes blasting into the store and nearly tackles me in a hug.

"Willow. What are you doing here?"

Logan is behind her, shuffling into the store.

"Would you be able to take her over with you tonight for the welcome dinner? I've got physical therapy this afternoon that I can't miss."

"Where are Mason and Ivy?"

"They had to go pick up some things in Jackson this afternoon."

"Really?" I cross my arms, giving my brother an assessing look. "Supplies?"

"Gross, Layla." Logan winces. "Mason had to get more wood to help build the altar for the wedding and Ivy went with him. I forgot I had my appointment when I told them I'd pick up Willow."

"How's the leg feeling today?"

"Sore."

"Is it good to go then?"

"I'll be fine," he grumbles.

After Logan's injury last year, I know he's tired of all of us hovering over him, making sure he's okay. But with the extent of the damage to his leg? We can't help but worry. He hasn't played a single game of football since, and I know it's starting to make him anxious. He's ready to get back out on the field.

"Do you want me to pick you up on my way over?"

He shakes his head. "I'm good. I'll see you guys there. Bye, Willow!"

"Bye, Uncle Logan!" She waves at him from where she's inspecting the latest jewelry. "Aunt Layla, can we work on my sewing project?" Willow's curls bounce in excitement.

"Of course we can."

The store is slow today. After a few rainy days, everyone is out enjoying the sunshine. I let Erica know where I'll be before I follow Willow into my workspace.

"Is that Aunt Gemma's dress?" Willow points to the mostly finished dress in the corner.

"It is. Isn't it pretty?"

Willow goes over to inspect it, knowing not to touch it from the other times she's been here.

"It looks like a dress now."

"Want to work on your dress?"

"Yes!"

When Gemma asked me to make her dress for the wedding, I took it one step further. I've been working on the bridesmaid dresses for Ivy and myself to match the groomsmen colors—a deep burgundy that will look gorgeous on a summer night. And with Willow being the flower girl, I'm making her dress.

With her help, of course, since she wants to help with everything her aunts do.

"Remember how to thread the sewing machine?"

"Yes."

"Grab your thread and let's get started."

Willow talks herself through how to thread the machine, her tongue sticking out in concentration. "Is that right?"

I nod. "Good job. We can finish the skirt, and then I think we need to get you home to get changed for the party tonight."

"Yes! I love going to fancy parties. I can't wait to wear this dress to the wedding."

"You'll look beautiful." I drop a kiss on her head. "Now, let's get sewing so you have something to wear."

Willow is precise in how slow she goes, careful not to make any mistakes. She's a natural at this. Maybe there will be another creator in the family.

As we finish off the last stitches, Erica pops her head in.

"Layla. Sorry to interrupt, but Mrs. Bush is here and needs to speak to you. Says it's important."

"Again?" Great. Just who I wanted to deal with today. "I'll be right back, Willow." I turn off the sewing machine. "No using this, got it?"

"Got it."

Pasting on my fakest, brightest smile, I head out into the shop. Mrs. Bush stands by the door in a perfectly pressed gray suit. It's about as drab as it can be.

"Mrs. Bush. What brings you by today?"

She hands me a stack of papers. "We will be reviewing the future use of this space at the next town council meeting."

She does not mince her words.

"I'm sorry, what?"

Gaze flying over the page, I try to find the most important parts to focus on. Like the fact that the meeting is only a few days before my sister's wedding. It also catches on *the future use of this space.*

"How did it go from not getting the Reynolds building to now deciding the future of Pinstripes & Push-Ups?"

"The mayor wants to be sure we have suitable businesses in Dixon that support our main form of income—tourism."

"The mayor or you?"

She huffs, straightening her jacket. "I am merely relaying what the mayor wants."

Mayor, my ass.

As much as I can't stand my ex-husband, this is her doing.

"I need a meeting with the mayor."

"Absolutely not." She shakes her head. That helmet hair of hers does not move an inch.

"You're telling me that you're deciding on the future of my business and I can't get two minutes to speak to the mayor? That's ludicrous."

"Maybe if you spent more time on a suitable business, this wouldn't be an issue."

The papers crunch into a ball in my hand, as I try to calm the anger surging through me at this woman.

"And what would you consider a *suitable* business, hmm?"

She studies the store, almost as if she is going to be the next renter of this space. "I think a craft store would fit in here nicely."

"A craft store. How does that help support tourism?"

"It doesn't need to support tourism. It can support the town."

"And I don't support the town by providing clothes?"

"Not the kind people should be wearing."

This conversation is getting us nowhere. She makes it

sound like people are gallivanting around town in just their underwear.

Anger courses through me. I hate how small-minded this woman is. I have been nothing short of an upstanding business owner. With the town owning half the buildings on Main Street, I go to every meeting, volunteer to be on committees I don't want to be on—all in the name of supporting the town and my business.

"Fine. Then I will be sure to be at the next meeting."

Mrs. Bush's lips pull into a thin line, practically disappearing into her face. "We will see you there."

There's a pep to her step as she leaves the store. I look down at the outfit I'm wearing—a skinny-strapped leopard-print camisole with ripped black jeans. Maybe if I dressed more like her, acted more like her, she would deem me suitable to run this place.

But one thing is for sure.

I'm not backing down without a fight.

Chapter Five

"**E**veryone has their assignments?" I look around at my team of five that I brought over for the month to provide security for the Davies families. Two are new hires, but the rest are my most trusted men.

"Yes, sir."

"Good. I'll keep you posted of any schedule changes." I check my watch. "They'll be arriving any minute, so head to your posts. Keep your radios on at all times."

We were given a suite in the main lodge to be on-site twenty-four seven. It's one of the smaller rooms, but it will fit all of the equipment we need for added security.

As my eyes do one final sweep of feeds from the security cameras I set up, I can't help but laugh when I get to the ones of the barn, remembering my first day here.

I can't say I've ever been accused of being a paparazzo before. Although I wouldn't mind another run-in with Gemma's sister.

I knew who she was before she introduced herself. I ran background checks on everyone so I was aware of exactly who we would be dealing with. It's standard protocol for any job I take.

I just never expected Layla to be as fiery as she is.

Grabbing my own radio, I head downstairs. The noise that greets me tells me the guests have arrived. With so many arriving at different times, a gourmet buffet of sorts was set up in the main restaurant before cocktails later tonight.

A group of children are munching on snacks on the couches while the adults are sipping drinks near the bar.

"Simon. How are you?" Charlotte calls me over, greeting me with a kiss on each cheek.

"Good. How was the flight over?"

"Harder with kids. Neither one of them likes to sit still."

"No doubt Pierce made it harder too." I laugh.

"Oy. I take offense to that," the man in question pipes up. "I was up for thirteen hours with Mary. She wouldn't sleep the entire flight."

Charlotte drops a peck on his cheek. "I'm sorry, love. I can't help that she's a daddy's girl."

"If I hear one more song about watermelons, I might go crazy," Pierce tells me.

"Watermelons?"

"When you have children, you'll understand." He waves me off. "How's everything looking around here?"

Reaching around him, I grab a water from the bar.

"You on the clock tonight?" Pierce asks.

"Just for dinner. Figured an extra set of eyes can never hurt."

"And is all well so far?"

Aside from the run-in with his sexy cousin?

Yes. But I don't tell him that.

My lips quirk up in a smile. "So far, no paparazzi in

town, but you know that could change in the blink of an eye. I have everyone on set shifts, rotating a few days out for rest."

"Did you give everyone the shit shifts?" Pierce sips on his beer.

"You're such a wanker. Just because you give people the shit shifts at the studio…"

"I do not!" He's affronted at the accusation. "We're not open late enough for shit shifts. These guys will be on all night."

"If it means keeping the paps out, then so be it."

Travel plans were kept under wraps, so it should be an easy few weeks. I've seen the jobs their London security team plays to keep them at bay.

Charlotte is a natural with the press. They eat her up, so they follow her everywhere they can. I'm thankful I'm only on duty for vacations. Working for them in London would be my only job.

And not something I'd want to do since Pierce is a friend.

Watching as more guests come downstairs for dinner, I'm momentarily distracted as a familiar blonde strides inside the restaurant. My eyes track her every move. All that blonde hair makes her look like an angel with the sun beaming inside.

As Layla spins on her heel, she notices us in the bar. Those blue eyes of hers trail over me. I sip my water, letting her take her fill.

When her gaze meets mine, I give her a cunning smile. She raises one brow in my direction before someone else grabs her attention.

Damn. This woman. I've met her for a grand total of ten minutes and I want to know more.

"Are you paying attention, mate?" Pierce snaps his fingers in front of my face.

"You were talking about singing watermelons?"

"What's got your attention?" He looks around and soon Charlotte and Layla are at his side.

"Simon. Have you met our cousin Layla?" Charlotte introduces me to her again.

She looks more incredible than she did the other day. She's wearing a black, V-neck dress that dips low. A gold necklace draws my eyes to the swell of her breasts.

Christ. How is this woman still single?

She's fucking stunning.

"Oh, we've met." Layla extends her hand, a blush creeping up her cheeks, no doubt remembering our exchange in the barn.

I wonder if that blush is everywhere.

"Layla. Always a pleasure." I take her hand, dropping a kiss on the back.

"How's security shaping up?" Layla asks, sipping on a glass of champagne.

"Better now that I had a consultant help with the barn."

"I'm sure they did a fine job helping you."

"Aren't you the security consultant?" Pierce interrupts.

"Nothing you need to worry about, mate." I clap him on the shoulder. "Layla's been a big help while I've been here."

"You have?" Pierce asks her.

Christ. This man is oblivious sometimes.

Layla shrugs her shoulder. "Who better to help than someone who knows this place inside out?"

Charlotte loops her arm through Layla's. "Let's leave these two be. I want to hear more about your store."

"I'm sure I'll be seeing you at The Tipsy Cocktail later?" she asks me as Charlotte pulls her over to see Ellie.

"I'll be there."

As if there would be any other place I'd go.

I want to know more about this woman.

And I'll take it any way I can get it.

Chapter Six

The Tipsy Cocktail is hopping tonight. With the welcome dinner behind us, Blake and Gemma wanted to end the evening in a more relaxed atmosphere with just the younger generation.

Likely because they didn't want Blake's stuck-up mother to come. I spent five minutes with the woman and it was worse than spending it with Mrs. Bush. Or Brad.

The door opens and my entire body prickles with awareness. Stepping inside after my cousins and their wives is Simon.

Private security Simon. Not a paparazzo Simon.

His eyes scan the crowd. When they cross over me, he does a double take.

I sip on my drink—the Clara, the bar's most popular drink—and try to look unaffected at his stare. I should be embarrassed at how I acted when I first met him, but when his eyes stay locked on mine? It's hard to care.

There's something there with Simon. A pull low in my belly. Something I haven't felt in a long time. Even after my divorce when I tried dating again, I didn't feel this.

Like there's a buzzing in my veins. Like every part of me wants to be near him. To feel him against me. To explore him.

"Hey, Layla."

I'm swept up in a whirl of pink.

"Ellie. I'm so happy you were able to make it."

She sweeps her bright pink hair off her shoulder. I've never met anyone that looks as beautiful as she does with hair like hers.

"We wouldn't have missed it. I can't believe Gemma is getting married."

I nod, sipping on my gingery drink. "Tell me about it. It seems like just yesterday Blake got to town."

Ellie flags down the bartender, ordering her own drink. "Speaking of coming to town…any plans on visiting us in London soon?"

"God, I wish. I miss it, but it's too hard to leave the shop."

Ellie grabs my arm. "I have got to stop by this week. I keep seeing all this fab lingerie you're posting and it's gorgeous. Where are you getting it from?"

"I make it."

"You do? How did I not know this?" she asks, appalled.

"You've got your hands full with the foundation and two kids."

"Don't forget about that husband of yours." Sean appears behind her, wrapping an arm around her shoulders.

"He might be the most work of all."

"You love it." He nips at her jaw.

It seems love is in the air. Everywhere I go, everyone is all loved up. Maybe it's the wedding making people extra sappy, but it's at times like this that I'm reminded of how painfully single I am.

Not that it's *not* by choice. I haven't found a good man worthy of settling down. I made that mistake once. Never again.

Speaking of which…Brad is lingering at the far end of the bar.

Swallowing down the last of my drink, I stand. "I'll be right back. I need a quick minute with our esteemed mayor."

Sean's eyes dart behind me and back. "You going to be alright?"

"It's him you should be worried about."

"What's going on?" Ellie asks as I stalk toward my ex-husband.

"What are you doing here, Brad? This is supposed to be a private affair tonight."

His eyes rake me over from head to toe. With him sitting, I'm taller than he is. It gives me the courage to have this conversation with him.

Having to discuss business with your ex is never fun.

"I only stopped in to check on one of the town's better businesses. No harm in that."

"You couldn't have gone to one of the other restaurants in town?"

He shakes his head. "None have the Clara."

"Yes they do."

"But no one makes it like The Tipsy Cocktail does."

Why are ex-husbands so terrible?

"Whatever." I wave him off. "Why do you keep ignoring my calls to set up a meeting?"

"A meeting for what?" Brad's face shows no sign that he knows what I'm talking about.

Fucker is already a good politician.

"To discuss getting the new space for Pinstripes & Push-Ups."

"Layla, do we have to discuss this tonight? I'm ready to leave work behind me for the night," Brad whines.

"Then why won't you return my calls?"

"It's a lost cause, Layla. Let it go."

I don't know what I ever saw in this man. Young and starry-eyed, maybe it was because he was the first man to give me any sort of attention. I was smitten from the start.

Now I can't believe I ever married someone who didn't support my dreams—no matter how unconventional they are.

"Why? Just because Mrs. Bush doesn't think I'm running a business suitable to her beliefs?"

"Because she thinks it's improper that an unmarried woman sells lingerie. Do you know how much she complains? More than I care to listen." Brad knocks back the rest of his cocktail.

Simon enters my line of sight. My body is so in tune with his, and I barely know him. Yet, any time he gets near me, I know it. My body senses his presence.

Which triggers a harebrained idea to enter my mind.

"And what if I'm not single?"

Brad eyes me up and down.

"Since when have you been seeing someone?"

I make sure he sees my dramatic eye roll. "And why would you know anything about my dating life?"

"Does it make a difference if you are seeing someone?"

"You tell me." I cross my arms, not letting this man get under my skin any more than he already has. "Mrs. Bush seems to have an issue with me being single. I'm dating someone, not that it's any of *her* business."

"Oh yeah? Who?"

"Simon!" I wave him over. His eyebrows furrow in confusion.

"Layla. How are you?"

"Better now that you're here." I wrap an arm around his waist, feeling his body go stiff under my touch.

"What?"

"I was just telling Brad here how we're dating."

If he's confused about what I just said, his face isn't showing it. "Dating."

"You're dating her? Why would you do that?" Brad's face is gleeful.

That gets a rise out of Simon, who hasn't taken his eyes off me.

I'm holding my breath, waiting to see what his next move will be.

Tell me to bugger off? Or come to my rescue like a knight in shining armor?

Or punch Brad in the face?

I'm hoping for option three.

"Why is this wanker ruining date night?"

A smile pulls at the corner of his mouth as my breath leaves me in a rush.

Thank God.

"If it's a date night, where have you been all night?" Brad asks.

Simon loosens up, pulling me into his side. "What's it matter to you?"

The two are locked in a stare off. Neither of them is making a move. My eyes are darting back and forth between the two of them.

Brad blinks first.

"I'll leave you two be." He stands, tail tucked between his legs as he leaves.

"I'll be calling you to set up that meeting." My words leave no room for argument.

Simon takes the now empty seat, pulling me between his legs. He checks to make sure the coast is clear, that we're secluded in this quiet part of the bar. Everyone is with Blake and Gemma who have just made their entrance.

"So that's your ex-husband?"

I lean down on the bar on my elbow. "And how do you know that's my ex?"

"Aside from him being a complete wanker to you?"

I fight the grin at his words. "Aside from that."

Simon's arm drops down onto the bar. His fingers are inching closer to my elbow. Standing here like this, I want to feel his touch. Even the thought of it has me itching for more.

"I have a full dossier on everyone, love. Better safe than sorry."

I lean in closer to him. "And what does that dossier say about me?"

A bashful look comes over his face. "Do you want to know?"

This time, I close the distance between us, grabbing his forearm. A shock of heat courses through me. Simon's eyes are locked at the point of contact.

"Now I have to know."

Green eyes lock onto mine. "Layla Winchester. Thirty-two years old. Divorced. Local shop owner of Pinstripes & Push-Ups. Current dating status single."

Way to boil my life down to a few sad points.

I point a finger in his face. "I see this dossier is incorrect."

"What's incorrect?"

Taking a step closer, I correct him. "Current dating status no longer single."

His breath is warm against my cheek. "I stand corrected."

"And here I know nothing about you, boyfriend."

"Something you should know—I don't put out on the first date."

"Really?" I give him a slow survey. I want to test that theory. God, do I ever.

Simon moves in closer, his lips close to my ear. "No. But that's something you don't get to know until later."

It sends shivers down my spine. Heat gathers in my core at his words.

Until later.

There's a glimmer of hope that what I unintentionally pulled this man into won't be just for tonight.

"Do you know what you're getting yourself into with this?" Simon asks.

The crowd is starting to thin out. No doubt it's getting late.

"Meet me at my shop tomorrow and we can discuss this. Iron out the details."

Simon stands, straightening his cuffs. Every time I've seen him, he's been dressed impeccably. As someone who makes their living in fashion, it's more of a turn-on than it should be. But the way Simon fills out his suit?

I'd be crazy *not* to take notice of him.

"And where is your shop?"

I press up onto my toes, whispering into his ear.

"Why don't you use that dossier of yours and come find me?"

Chapter Seven

LAYLA

This is not a good idea. Quite possibly the worst one I've ever had. Convincing Simon to be my boyfriend to get Brad and Mrs. Bush—and this entire town—off my back during the wedding?

There's no way we'll be able to pull this off.

Now that the buzz of the alcohol has worn off, I'm thinking more clearly.

More clearly than I was last night.

I must be going crazy.

The clicking of the sewing machine bounces around the room as I push the material of Gemma's dress through. It's one of the only things I can focus on right now.

Sewing has always been able to quiet the noise of whatever is going on with my life. It was what kept me going after I left my ex.

And it was something he never fully supported.

A brisk knock echoes from the back door that leads directly into my workroom from the alley. No doubt it's Simon, coming to discuss my insane idea from the night before.

"It's open."

I pull the skirt out from the machine and cut the thread so I can place it back on the dress form where it's safe. The last thing I want is anything happening to this work in progress.

The door to my workroom swings open and there he is.

Simon in all his muscly glory.

Tight jeans meld to his thighs. The leather jacket he's wearing strains against his muscles.

Those biceps? He could probably snap a person like a twig. The thought shouldn't make my stomach flutter and my thighs clench together, but it does.

Why does he look even more attractive like this?

Snapping my resolve into place, I push back from my sewing machine and cross one leg over the other. I watch as Simon's eyes follow my leg, a slow perusal as he takes me in.

I'm thankful that I always put effort into how I look. No matter if I'm in the store or in the workroom, I like looking put together.

With a white fitted crop top and overalls, it's simple, yet has Simon taking his fill.

Huh. I guess I'm not the only one intrigued by the other person in this arrangement.

"Looks like you used that dossier of yours."

"It seems I did." He quirks a brow at me before turning his gaze around my small studio.

As far as workspaces go, it's nothing fancy. Female dress forms line the room, all with half-finished pieces from the fall's new line. A corkboard hangs on the wall facing me with all the ideas I have for the store and my lingerie collection. Spools of fabric and thread cover every spare surface.

"This is where you work?"

"It is."

"And it's only you making all this?" He walks over to where I have a top pinned onto the form. I dropped everything to make Gemma's wedding dress.

I wiggle my fingers in front of him. "I'm good with my hands."

"Is that so?"

Dropping my elbows on the worktable, I clasp my fingers and place my chin on my hands. "Not sure if that's something that would be in that little file of yours."

"You're quite interested in this dossier, love."

I give Simon my biggest smile. "Look at you. Calling me love. Already we're a match made in heaven."

He laughs, low and deep. It's a sound I could get used to.

Simon shrugs out of his jacket, dropping it on the love seat I have back here. It's small, but cozy.

"Tell me why I should go through with this."

I knew this was coming. Simon has every right to think I'm crazy. First I accuse him of being a paparazzo. Then I pull him into some crazy scheme to be my boyfriend.

"Come with me." Opening the door to the main shop, I shoo Simon in front of me. The store has long since closed. "This place is my entire life."

I watch as Simon takes an assessing sweep of the space. Old chandeliers hang from the ceiling. Racks of clothes fill the space. Lingerie from my new collection is on tables in the back near the dressing rooms. Purple oversized chairs sit in front of the black and white striped wallpaper. The store's sign hangs in the middle of the wall—the perfect focal point.

"Pinstripes & Push-Ups is everything to me. The way people always leave here feeling beautiful. Empowered. I love knowing I did that. It got me through my divorce. I can't lose it because some people in town don't deem it an appropriate business for a woman."

Simon turns, dropping into one of the two chairs. He crosses his legs at his ankles, giving me an assessing stare. "And you think pretending to date is going to make all those people go away?"

"Maybe? I see the looks they give me. It's like I can't be an accomplished woman unless I have a man on my arm."

Simon scoffs. "That's a bit old-fashioned, isn't it?"

I give him a fake smile. "That's what being in a small town gets you."

"Christ. I can't imagine that."

His accent is thick and delicious. I could sit here and listen to it for hours. Why I'm asking the most attractive man I've met in ages to do this for me, I don't know. Maybe I should be rethinking it because of that small fact.

"It's my reality. And if I have to pretend for a few weeks to make it look like I have my life together, then so be it."

Simon leans closer. Up close, I can see flecks of gold reflecting in his green eyes. "And what happens when I go back to London?"

"Ever heard of long-distance?"

"You've got this all figured out, don't you?"

I laugh. "Considering it came to me about, oh, twenty-four hours ago, I'm thinking on the fly here."

Simon taps his fingers on the velvet of the chair. It's the only sign that he's thinking this over. Everything about him seems so intentional and purposeful. I guess that comes with the territory of being a bodyguard.

"What do you need from me to make this work?"

I blow out a breath I didn't realize I was holding. "Considering I'll need a date to all the wedding events, it'll be a lot."

"Okay." He nods his head.

"And some dates around town. Just to make it seem real."

"Okay."

"That's it? Okay?"

"What? Do you want me to be more difficult, love?"

Love. There is that word is again. Why do I love hearing that roll off his tongue so much?

"No, I don't. Does this mean you're agreeing to it?"

Simon pushes up off the chair, coming to stand in front of me. He holds out a hand, pulling me up.

"Yes, I am, Layla. I will be your fake boyfriend. And whatever else that entails."

"Simon. Thank you."

My eyes drift past him, glancing around my store. This is the reason I'm doing this. To make sure the people of this town deem me worthy of running a store that helps others feel beautiful.

"We'll need to swap numbers."

"Look at you, asking for my number already." I try to add some levity. Now that Simon has agreed, things just got a lot more real.

"I like getting numbers from all of the pretty girls."

"All?" I quirk a brow at him. "Will I have a *real* girl-friend back home in London to compete with?"

I hold my breath waiting for his answer. If Simon has a girlfriend, this whole thing is off. I don't want to get in the middle and make things messy for him.

"I wouldn't have said yes if that were the case."

"I'm glad my boyfriend is a stand-up guy then."

Simon steps closer, his tea and lemon scent invading my senses. "Do you need me to bring you some roses to really seal the deal?"

"No roses. Not my thing."

"Guess I'll have to get creative then."

The silence of the store is loud around us. I can't believe this man is going to help me save this place.

I have no idea if this slightly insane and desperate plan will work. It could succeed, or it could ruin everything. I don't know what's going to happen, but I know I couldn't do it without Simon who is so willingly stepping up to help.

"And will this interfere with your schedule?" I ask.

Simon shakes his head. "No. We have rotating schedules. I will make myself available to you whenever you need. Besides, it won't hurt to have an extra set of eyes at the wedding functions."

"I'm glad that it will be of help to you then."

"Just wait until Pierce hears about this," he says on a laugh.

"No!" I bite out. "We can't tell anyone. I know Pierce is your best friend, but he has the biggest mouth, and I don't want this getting out."

"Will you be able to keep it to yourself then?"

I nod with a little too much force. "It's the only way this will work."

Even if it means lying to my family. They'll understand, right?

"Right. And if people ask how we met?"

"London." I'm quick to answer. "I've visited my family there a few times. We can easily play it off."

Simon gives me a soft smile. "I guess you've thought of everything then."

"Mostly. Can I ask you something?"

"Considering you've been full of questions tonight..."

I smack him on the chest. Simon is a full head taller than I am. He has an air about him—an overwhelming presence in the very best way.

"Why are you doing this?"

There's Simon's laugh again. It's the sweetest sound. Something I could get used to hearing. "Are you trying to talk me out of this? I've already said yes."

"Not at all." I shake my head. "But you're agreeing to this after I accused you of being here to stalk my family. You could have easily told me to go to hell."

Simon tucks a stray lock of hair behind my ear. "I have my reasons."

"Will I ever get to hear them?"

"Maybe."

"Shouldn't you tell your girlfriend these things?"

"My girlfriend is awfully demanding."

I cross my arms, standing as tall as I can. "I can't help it if you know everything about me and I know nothing about you."

"I like trains. Does that satisfy your need for information?"

I roll my eyes at him. "Hardly."

"Do I get to ask you a question now?"

I fight the smile threatening to split my face wide open. If this is what the next few weeks will be like, this might not be so bad.

"Go ahead."

"Layla, love, will you go out on a date with me?"

Oh yeah, I'm going to really enjoy these next few weeks.

Chapter Eight

"Do I look okay?" I turn in the mirror, asking my cat.

Is this really what my life has come to? Talking to my cat and asking for fashion advice for my first date with my fake boyfriend?

Luna yawns, returning to licking her paw.

"Lot of help you are," I mutter.

Spinning back to the mirror, I give myself another appraising look. I paired my denim cut-off shorts with a white blouse and white sneakers. It's perfect for the summer nights here in Dixon.

Simple, yet appropriate for a first date in town.

Thinking about the date has nerves twisting my stomach. I can't remember the last time I've been out on a first date. Sure, I had a few dates here and there after my divorce, but I didn't count them as dates.

There were no nerves, no pressure. I went into them knowing nothing would come of them. I wasn't looking for love then. I'm still not.

Then why am I so nervous for tonight?

A knock on my door echoes through the quiet apartment. Luna makes no move to get up from the bed, instead burrowing under the duvet.

Swiping one last layer of lip gloss on, I spritz myself with perfume and head to the door. Taking a centering breath, I open the door to Simon.

He looks casual in a plaid, short-sleeve button-up and jeans. But it's the look in his eyes as they travel over me that sets me on fire.

Because Simon is looking at me like he is ready to devour me.

"You look beautiful, Layla." Simon leans in, dropping a kiss on my cheek. It sends more nerves racing through me.

"Thank you. You don't look so bad yourself."

He runs a hand down his shirt. "Like I fit in with the locals?"

"Is that the look you're going for?" I grab my purse from the counter and step out the door.

"I ran into Blake as I was leaving and he told me the leather jacket might be too grungy."

I laugh. "Of course Blake is helping you try to fit in." I lock the door behind me.

He shrugs a shoulder as I follow him down the stairs onto the main drag. "Hey, if it helps you, then I'm all for it."

The comment brings me back to reality.

Simon is helping my reputation to make sure I don't lose my shop. Nothing more, nothing less.

"Where are we going tonight?"

"How about Dixon Bar and Grill? Fewer prying eyes from family."

I laugh as we walk in that direction. "You've been around the Winchester family for all of a week and you've already pegged us. Peter wouldn't leave us alone if we went to The Tipsy Cocktail."

Simon reaches for my hand, linking it with his. A zap of electricity shoots up my arm.

"Hand-holding?" I suck in a breath.

"It's what couples do, love."

"Right."

"Need to make it believable." Simon bumps me with his elbow.

"Then if we're going to make this believable, I think it's time I know more about my boyfriend."

"What do you want to know?"

Arriving at the restaurant, Simon grabs the door and holds it open for me. Couples and families are spread out among all the tables. Old sitcoms play on the TVs lining the bar. The hostess grabs two menus for us and shows us to a high-top table in the middle of the bar.

I don't miss the gazes tracking us as we follow her through the restaurant. As much as I hate all the attention on me, it's what we need to make this believable.

"Your server will be with you shortly."

"What's good here?" Simon asks, leaning back in his chair. He looks relaxed here. Like he's always been a part of this town.

"Get the burger. You can never go wrong with that."

"Hmm." He eyes the menu, deliberately taking his time.

"Are you stalling?" I drum my fingers on the table as he continues to consider what to get for dinner.

"Stalling?"

"Clearly someone doesn't like talking about themselves."

He quirks a brow at me. "Just checking out all my options."

"Welcome to the Dixon Bar and Grill. What can I get you tonight?"

"Two medium burgers and two Claras, please."

"Be right back." Our server is gone as fast as they came.

"We're at the point in our relationship where you're ordering for me?"

"Only when you're being evasive."

"I like a woman that takes charge." Simon winks at me. Resting his arms on the table, he leans closer to me. "What do you want to know?"

"Do you have any siblings?"

"Just me."

"Was it lonely being an only child?"

Simon shrugs a shoulder. "I had my people."

"Who were your people?"

It's then I notice two people approaching us out of the corner of my eye.

"Shit."

"What?" Simon looks around immediately. The body-guard in him is probably looking for the closest threat. Not that he would notice it in the two white-haired women walking our way.

"Layla. How nice to see you out."

"Mrs. Bush. Mrs. Lewis. How nice to see you both." I reach across the table, clasping Simon's forearm.

This is exactly why I needed Simon.

"Who is this strapping young gentleman you have with you?" Mrs. Lewis turns to Simon, taking him in. No doubt she's trying to glean anything she can from him from this brief meeting.

"This is Simon Belvy. My boyfriend."

"Boyfriend? Since when do you have a boyfriend?"

Mrs. Bush looks shocked at my words. "You haven't been dating."

"Because she's been dating me," Simon answers for me.

"Seems like an odd pairing." Mrs. Bush's eyes travel between the two of us.

Is it wrong to want to smack an old woman? I've disliked this woman since the third grade when she told me off for coloring too much on my schoolwork. Not that it wasn't warranted, but she's been rude to me ever since.

I haven't had enough to drink to deal with them yet.

"I'm going to go check on those drinks." Simon drops a peck on my cheek before heading to the bar.

Thank you, I mouth as he winks back at me.

I watch as he walks away. The way his strong legs eat up the distance. The way his muscles flex under his shirt.

Every part of him is sexy.

"What a gentleman. Getting your drinks for you."

I try not to roll my eyes. "He's a keeper."

"And how did you meet him?" Mrs. Lewis asks.

"In London."

"How does dating work like that? Not much of a relationship, is it?" Mrs. Bush questions. "I can't imagine it's going to last. You need a man close by if you're going to keep him around."

"She couldn't even keep the mayor. A fine, upstanding citizen like him." Mrs. Lewis tuts. "I don't foresee this lasting at all."

"And with the cavalier way she runs her business?" Mrs. Bush shakes her head. "I'm surprised she even found him."

"A single woman over thirty? She'll probably be an old maid at our age."

Their condescending tone is the last straw.

"Well, you don't need to worry about it lasting," I snap. These two…talking about me like I'm not even here.

"And why's that, dear?" Mrs. Bush uses her teacher voice, like she's trying to appease my outburst.

"Because we're engaged!"

Wide eyes look at me as I process what I just yelled.

So much for a fake boyfriend. Looks like I have myself a fake fiancé now.

Where is Simon with those drinks when I need one?

Chapter Nine

"**B**ecause we're engaged!" Layla shouts.

"You're what?" one of the old women standing by our table gasps.

"That's right. He's my fiancé."

"Since when?" the other woman asks, her face skeptical.

Not a single one of them have noticed me standing in the shadows. I'd like to hear her answer to this as well.

"Since, uh…since…" From the limited time I've known Layla, nothing gets to her. This whole fake dating thing was a means to an end for her. To keep her shop and get the town off her back. Now she's rattled.

"Since her last trip to London." I step in, setting the drinks down and wrapping an arm around her waist, pulling her back into me. Her blue eyes turn up to find mine, panic written all over her face.

"When were you last in London?" one of the two women asks. For fuck's sake they're nosy.

"April. Would you like a copy of her travel itinerary to confirm?"

"You said you were going to visit your parents in April," one of them says to Layla with a questioning gaze.

Fuck, that was lucky.

"Like I said, April. We've been keeping it under wraps because we didn't want to take focus away from Gemma."

"And where's the ring?"

"It's being resized. It's tucked safely away at a jewelry store back home."

"It's beautiful. I'll be sure to show you the next time I have it on," Layla tells them, resting a hand on my abs. A shock of heat races through me at her soft touch. She must feel it too because her fingers dig even farther into me.

"How did he pop the question?"

"Can't we keep some things to ourselves?" I ask them.

It's the wrong thing, as they start to go off on me.

"Are they always like this?" I bend down closer so they can't hear me.

Layla turns to face me, a tight smile baring her gritted teeth. "Yes. Now you understand why."

I tuck a stray lock of blonde hair behind her ear. This close, I can make out the faint freckles dusted across the bridge of her nose. The way her blue eyes give way to gray.

Fucking hell, this woman is gorgeous. Should I really have agreed to fake date—now I guess fake marry—someone that I'm actually attracted to?

Not one of my better ideas.

My eyes don't leave Layla's. "I proposed at St. Dunstan's. It's a quiet spot in London. Layla doesn't like the touristy spots in the city, so I took her there."

She's biting her lip now, almost like she's waiting to hear where this goes.

"We snuck in just before it closed and were the only ones there. She was leaving the next day and I just couldn't let her leave without asking her to marry me. I didn't care that we'd only met last summer. I couldn't lose this woman. She's my everything."

Layla sucks in a breath at my last words. Her eyes widen, not straying from mine. The noise of the bar dims around us. It's like we're the only two people here.

It would be so easy to kiss her right now. To close the distance between the two of us and see what she tastes like.

Does she taste like that sugary lip balm she put on earlier? No doubt she'll taste as good as she smells. Whatever perfume she's wearing hits me right below the belt.

Everything about this woman is seductive, pulling me into a trance.

Fuck, do I ever want to find out how she tastes, but we never discussed PDA. Sure, hand-holding and light touching to make it seem believable.

Except…is Layla getting closer? All I can think about now is kissing her.

"Hmm. Well, they certainly seem to be in love."

The voice breaks through the fog, causing us to jump apart.

"Layla. Simon. Have a nice evening."

"About time they left." Layla grabs her drink and chugs half of it as soon as they're gone.

The noise of the bar comes back to life. It's not as crowded now as it was before.

"I'm your fiancé now, hmm?" I cross my arms, staring down at Layla. I don't give her any space. We're still as close as before.

A spot I don't mind being in.

"It was the only thing I could think of."

"And here I thought I'd get lucky before getting engaged."

"Stop it."

"Am I allowed to see you before the wedding? Have we decided that yet?"

"And I'm dumping you." Layla rolls her eyes at me.

I look at my watch in jest. "Shortest relationship to date. Damn, Layla."

Layla takes a smaller sip of her drink as our server sets our plates down on the table. "I panicked, okay? They kept firing all these questions at me about you and they acted like they didn't believe me."

"Can't imagine why."

This gets me a laugh. "I'm sorry. The one on the left there"—Layla points behind her, my eyes tracking her movement—"was my third grade teacher. She's hated me ever since."

"Christ, as a kid? What'd you do to get on her bad side?" I grab my drink, taking my own sip. Damn, that shit is good.

"I was never the best student. I'd rather be coloring or dressing up my dolls than be doing my math tables."

"That's a long time to hold a grudge."

Layla laughs, a deep silky sound that I wouldn't mind hearing more. "What can I say? I never toed the line."

"So you've always been the rebel?"

"I guess you could say that."

Layla looks calmer than she did earlier. I don't know if it's the alcohol buzzing in her veins, or the act we put on. I do know one thing for certain, though. She needs me.

"Christ, no wonder you needed my help." I scrub a hand down my face, reaching for my dinner.

"At least it's only for a few weeks," she reminds me.

One day or a few years, any amount of time is fine.

I don't mind being Layla's fake anything. Because fuck, this woman is the real deal.

Chapter Ten

LAYLA

"**A**re you sure you're ready for this?" I can't help but ask Simon again. After how the other night turned out, I expected him to run.

Agreeing to be my fake boyfriend is one thing. But my fake fiancé? That's something completely different.

And this afternoon is the first event since our *engagement* where we'll be around my whole family.

It's enough to make me turn and run.

"Has anyone told you that you worry too much?" Simon's lips pull up in a smirk. This seems to be a tell of his.

"Doing this in front of the town is one thing. Convincing my family? Entirely different story," I mutter, more to myself than anything.

Simon pulls me up short, not letting me head to the picnic with just the Winchester family.

"You don't think they'll believe us?"

"We're going to have to sell it."

Simon cups my cheek in his strong hand. My skin heats immediately at his touch. He drops his head closer to mine.

His lips are so close, I could press up on my toes and kiss him.

"I think we did a pretty good job selling this the other night, no?"

Considering we got Mrs. Bush to back off, I'd say we did a good job of it.

"It's okay to admit it. I'm very easy to like."

"Stop it." I push Simon off me, but his playfulness helps cut the tension inside me.

"C'mon, love." Simon wraps his arm around my shoulder and pulls me down the trail to where the cookout is. "I have some Winchesters to impress."

Easier said than done.

Walking around to the field behind the lodge, we find everything done up perfectly. Over the last few months, Gemma has been making sure the ranch is in tip-top shape for her wedding. Not that it is ever in disrepair, but if there was even a dot of paint needing to be touched up, it's been done.

String lights crisscross overhead as Old Betty—Gramps's infamous red truck—is filled to the brim with ice and drinks in its bed. One of the local BBQ joints is serving up every kind of meat you can think of.

It smells delicious out here.

"What the hell are you two doing together?" Pierce draws up short as he sees the two of us, still standing on the outer fringes of the group.

"Nice to see you too, mate." Simon punches his shoulder.

"Why are you two together?" He wags a finger between the two of us, confusion drawing his brows together.

"I think we're going to blow his mind," Simon whispers into my ear so only I can hear.

"We're dating," I tell Pierce, matter-of-factly.

"No fucking way. I'd know if my best mate was dating someone."

"Not dating." Simon drops his hold on me and links his hand with mine. "Engaged."

Pierce just blinks back at the two of us. Stunned would be the word to describe him.

"I think we broke him," I whisper to Simon.

"We definitely did. Should we just leave him here?"

"Fuck off, you two. This is all some big joke."

Simon squeezes my hand. It's a show of solidarity, but it makes me feel like I have a true partner in this.

"Not a joke, Pierce."

"But…how? Just…how?" His eyes keep darting back and forth between the two of us, looking more and more confused.

It's at that moment Gemma chooses to come over to us.

"Oh boy."

"Hey…" Her eyes immediately zero in on Simon's and my joined hands. "What are you two doing?"

"Can't a girl bring her boyfriend to family dinner?" My voice is casual, not betraying the nerves that are now pumping through me.

Faking this thing to the town is one thing. To my family, that I'm close with? It's going to be one of the hardest things I've ever done.

I only hope they can forgive me for lying to them when all is said and done.

"Wait, what?" Gemma looks as stunned as Pierce was only moments ago. "You're not dating anyone."

"Ouch." Simon forces some hurt into his voice, but when I look up at him, he gives me a wink.

"I tried setting you up a few weeks ago and you said you were on a self-imposed dating hiatus."

"Because I was dating him"—I point to Simon—"and it would've been bad to say yes to a date when you're already with someone."

"Dating? Tell them what you really are," Pierce interrupts.

"What's that?" Gemma turns to him.

"Fiancées. They are engaged."

"Thank you, Pierce, you're so helpful." I give him a fake smile.

"You're engaged?!" Gemma's voice is a screech over the low noise of activity. "Actually engaged?"

"Can we not do this here?" I wince. Inquisitive eyes turn in our direction.

"You didn't tell me you got engaged!" Gemma's fuming. I wouldn't be surprised if smoke started coming out of her ears. My sister is not one to get mad. She's probably the most even-keeled Winchester.

But now? I don't think I've ever seen her so mad.

"You're engaged? Since when?" Logan walks up. His pace is slow with rehab pushing him harder and harder. He sips his beer, eyeing the two of us.

"How's your leg feeling?" I try to deflect the conversation off me.

Gemma waves a hand in front of him. "Oh no. Logan can wait. You'll see him later."

"Gee, thanks Gem," he scoffs.

She rolls her eyes at him in the way only a little sister can. "Don't you want to know all about Layla's *engagement*?"

Logan's eyes drift back to mine. "Yeah, when *did* this happen? And who is said fiancé?"

Simon reaches across me, extending his hand to my brother. "Simon Belvy. The fiancé in question."

"Okay. We have the who. How about the when?" Gemma asks, crossing her arms.

"I need a drink for this."

"Want me to go get you something, love?"

He starts to leave, but I grab him by his perfectly crisp white shirt. "Don't leave me."

"Everything okay over here?" Blake joins the fray now.

"My sister is engaged."

"Which sister?" he asks, looking confused.

"This sister." I hold up my hand. "She only has one."

"No, you're not. We'd know if you were engaged." Blake looks to Gemma to confirm what he's saying.

"Apparently not. She was just going to give us the details."

"Can I get a drink first?"

Everyone's eyes stay locked on mine.

"I'll be right back," Simon whispers.

My eyes track his movement. No one moves as he dashes over to the truck and pulls out two beers.

I can see why they're all stunned. After a marriage that ended in divorce, every move I make now is calculated. I've never wanted to rock the boat of my life or make a rash decision.

Me and my shop. That's all I've needed.

So now, with every set of eyes looking at me like I've lost my mind? I seek out the one person who is my calm.

Simon.

Someone I've only known a few days, but has been there with me every step of the way.

"Here you go, love."

I take a gulp of the icy beer, letting it calm my insides.

"Details, Layla. Details," Pierce says, clapping his hands in front of me.

"The last time I went to London." I'm as vague as possible.

"When was the last time you went to London?" This time it's Mason joining the circle.

"What are you, MI-6?" I ask.

"Aww, is your fiancé rubbing off on you?" Pierce's voice is dripping in sarcasm.

Our little bubble has drawn everyone's attention, because everyone has left what they're doing to come see what's going on.

"Did you know this was a thing?" Gemma turns to Pierce. "Why didn't you tell us?"

"Relax." He throws his hands up. "I only just found out like you did."

"Layla." Gemma fixes her deep brown eyes, so unlike my blue ones, on me. "This is not like you. A mysterious trip to London and now you're telling us you have a fiancé? What's going on?"

"She didn't want to take away from your wedding." Simon is quick to step in.

"There's 'not taking away from my wedding' and then there's just 'not telling us,' Layla."

Taking my sister's hand, I pull her aside. I feel everyone's eyes on us.

"I didn't want to hurt you. That was not my intention." I peek back over my shoulder. I ignore everyone and find Simon's eyes on me. He gives me the smallest of nods, encouraging me on. "It killed me not to tell you, but I know how excited you've been about the wedding."

"But you're my sister. You can always tell me these things. I haven't been some crazy bridezilla, right?"

"Well…" Mason chooses that moment to interrupt.

Thank God.

"I have not!"

"You yelled at me the other day because I ordered the wrong drinks."

"Because you were too busy making eyes at Ivy to notice."

A dopey smile comes over my brother's face at the mention of Ivy's name. Talk about a man in love.

"Yeah, that was my fault. You were right to be mad."

"See?" She turns back to me. "Not a bridezilla."

"If anyone, it's my mother," Blake tells everyone.

"Don't let her hear you say that." Gemma looks around, as if she'll pop out from around a corner any second.

"If our Layla is happy, then I'm happy." I spin on my heel and see Gramps standing on the outer part of the circle, no doubt taking in his big crazy family.

"You are?" I walk over to him, needing a hug from him.

"You look happy. And if this gentleman here makes you happy, that's all that matters."

I squeeze my eyes shut. It's hard to lie to my gramps. He was there for me more than anyone after my divorce. With my siblings in school and having their own lives, Gramps spent most weekends with me to make sure I was taken care of.

I don't know if I would have made it through without him.

"Mr. Winchester. It's a pleasure to meet you."

Simon extends his hand to my grandfather, who immediately takes it. "You take care of our Layla, ya hear?"

"Absolutely, sir."

Gramps smiles down at me. "Sir. I like him." Gramps claps his hands. "Now, it's time to eat."

Finally—*finally*—the crowd around us starts to dissolve. Blake pulls a weary Gemma over to the picnic tables where platters of food are being set out. Mason is standing close by, no doubt wanting to get his older brother two cents in.

"Feeling okay?" Simon steps over to me, enveloping me in a hug. I sink into his hold.

"That could've been a lot worse."

"Careful." Simon looks around. "You don't want them to hear if you don't want more questions."

I bark out a laugh. "Ready to run for it yet?"

"The only place I'm running is to the table. I'm fucking starving."

Pierce is still standing nearby, watching us with an eagle eye.

"I still don't understand this."

Simon rolls his eyes at him. "There's nothing to understand. We're in love and getting married. That's all you need to know."

"Okay."

"Why do you say it like that?" Simon throws back at him.

The two of them are in a stare down.

From everything Simon has told me, Pierce is his closest friend. The more I think about it, the more I realize this could affect not only my relationships, but Simon's too.

What were we thinking?

"Listen, Pierce. You might not understand this, but it's happening." Simon turns to face me. His green eyes are dark as they sweep over me. There's a stubble lining his jaw that wasn't there the other day.

Damn, if he's not the sexiest man I've ever laid eyes on.

"I love her. And I'll do anything to protect her. So I really hope you can be okay with this."

"Fuck, man." Pierce scrubs a hand down his face. "It came out of nowhere."

"I know." I step up to Simon's side. "And we didn't

want to spring it on everyone, but you know how this town is. They kept poking and bugging me about him—"

"And it just slipped out," Simon finishes.

"Holy shit. This is real," Mason says, startling us all. "I was with Pierce, not knowing what to think, but…"

"They are pretty cute together. It's the accent, isn't it?" Pierce jokes, walking over to Mason.

"What woman doesn't love an accent?" I laugh.

"Is that the only reason you're with me? I'm hurt."

"As long as you two aren't all gross and kissy, I'm fine with this," Mason tells us.

"Kissy?" I ask.

Mason shakes his head, laughing. "Willow. She doesn't like to see Ivy and me being 'kissy.'"

Simon holds up his hand like a Boy Scout. "I promise I will keep the kissy to a minimum."

"Good man." Mason gives him a firm nod. Not that I need my brother's approval, but I never had it with Brad. Maybe that should have been my first clue that the relationship wasn't going to last.

With Mason heading off, Simon throws an arm around Pierce.

"We good?"

"Of course, you wanker. I can never stay mad at you." He gives him a quick clap on the back before heading off in the direction of the food.

"Holy shit." I breathe a sigh of relief. I swallow a cool sip of beer, letting it calm my anxious nerves. "I think that went better than I could have expected."

"God, I hate to think what you truly thought was going to happen."

"Honestly? I thought fists would fly."

Simon looks horrified. "They would hit you?"

"God no! At you."

"Please. I can take them."

"Okay, Mr. Belvy. You did put on a rather good show tonight."

"I thought I was going to shit my pants when your granddad came over. I thought he'd be the hardest of the lot."

I shake my head, stepping away from him to lead him to the tables. "He's the easy one."

"Oh yeah? Anyone else easy?"

"Guess you'll have to find out."

Chapter Eleven

SIMON

"We're not prepared for this. I know nothing about you." Layla twists her hands in her lap as I pull into the ranch.

"Layla, love. You have got to stop worrying. It's going to be fine."

Dropping my hand over her clasped ones, she stills instantly. A warmth spreads through me at the innocent contact.

"It's a newlywed game night. How can I *not* worry?"

She turns those fierce blue eyes to mine.

"We don't have to know every little thing about one another." I put the truck I rented into park and turn to face Layla.

My fiancée now.

"But it has to look believable."

"You want my dossier?" I quirk a brow at her.

"Couldn't hurt. Especially since you have mine."

"It doesn't tell me the little things," I point out.

"Like Whitney Houston is one of my favorite singers? Or that watermelon Starburst are my favorite candy?"

"Watermelon?" My face screws up. "How can you like watermelon? Licorice Allsorts are my favorite."

Layla's face mirrors my own—a look of disgust. "Licorice? What are you, a serial killer? Who eats licorice?"

"I don't know if this relationship is going to work."

That gets a smile from her.

"Next you'll tell me you're a dog person."

I shake my head. "Cats. My grandparents had them growing up, so I like them."

"Acceptable." She nods her head at me, a lock of blonde hair falling in her face. It looks silky soft from here. It's hard to suppress the thoughts of what it would look like wrapped around my fist as I pound into her.

"Aside from questionable taste in music and candy—" I start, trying to get my brain back to more neutral thoughts, but get interrupted.

"Questionable?" Her voice goes high. "There is nothing wrong with Whitney Houston."

"She's not The Clash."

"Of course you like The Clash."

"Well, you probably don't watch football."

"You mean soccer?"

We should probably get inside, but I'm having too much fun learning about Layla. Poking and prodding to get a rise out of her.

"Football, love," I correct, "and the best team is Arsenal."

"You're right. I don't watch *your* football. My football team? Mountain Lions, no question."

I knew that without her having to tell me since her brother played for them.

"Looks like we can cheer for each other's teams then."

"Is that enough to get us through tonight?" She voices the question that I know is still plaguing her.

I hop out and circle around to Layla's side of the truck. Opening her door, she spins to face me. Her black shorts ride up her legs. All that exposed skin plays havoc with my mind, wondering what they'd feel like wrapped around me.

"Simon?" Layla snaps her fingers in front of me, a knowing look on her face.

"Right. You want me to tell them how you bite down on your lip when you're sewing? Or how you try to quirk up this eyebrow"—I rub a finger over her right one—"when you're annoyed, but you can't actually do it?"

"I don't do that," she protests.

"Sure you don't."

Like she's trying to do right now.

Pushing me back, Layla steps out of the truck, wearing heels that put her eye to eye with me.

"Another thing I know about you?"

"What's that?" She crosses her arms over her chest.

"That no matter where you go, you're always dressed to impress."

My eyes rake over her, from head to toe. From her perfectly made-up face, long blonde locks curling past her shoulders, and the light green top that hugs her curves.

Layla is a bombshell.

I don't know how else to put it.

Every man in this town is an idiot. Who wouldn't want to be with Layla?

I'm a right lucky bastard. Even if this is pretend. Getting to be in her world for a few weeks is better than not at all.

"Alright. Maybe we can pull this off." Layla links hands with me and pulls me behind her.

Soft murmurs of the gathering crowd inside the lodge

can be heard with the doors thrown open. Her hand tightens around mine as we walk into the open lobby.

Giving her a squeeze of reassurance back, I lean in closer to her. "Champagne to take the nerves off?"

She nods. "Please."

A bartender I haven't met yet—but have a full dossier on—is serving drinks.

"Pint of the lager and a glass of champagne, please."

"Coming right up."

"Simon. I didn't think you'd be here tonight." Sean comes up on my left, resting his elbow on the bar.

"And why wouldn't we?"

"Didn't think you'd want to get your ass handed to you in front of the whole family."

"And what makes you think I'm going to lose?"

Sean sips from his beer as Pierce sidles over to us.

"Who's losing what tonight? Are we betting?"

I take the beer from the bartender. "Cheers."

"I was just saying how nice it was that Simon came tonight when he'll likely be losing."

"Ouch, brother. Coming out with the trash talk."

Sean shrugs a shoulder. "Someone will be winning a bottle of Peter's new vodka. We have the night to ourselves and babysitting on the line."

"Babysitting?"

Pierce nods. "Fuck, yeah. Loser has to watch the other's kids for a whole month of nights out."

"This is what your lives have come to?" I laugh.

They both look horrified at what I've said.

"Do you know how hard it is to find a good babysitter?" Sean asks. "Never know people's true intentions."

"You know you could just ask your mother-in-law. I'm sure she has a list of people who are trustworthy."

"We're not bothering her with that. She has a country to run."

"Metaphorically," Pierce interjects.

"Besides"—Sean waves down the bartender for another drink—"Ellie doesn't like leaving the kids with strangers."

"So babysitting it is." Pierce makes a slashing motion over his throat. "You're going down, bro."

"In your dreams." Sean tells him, making the same move.

Christ. These people really are competitive.

"What's taking so long over here?" Layla sidles up to my side, slipping her arms around my waist.

"Just these two wanker cousins of yours."

"What are they up to now?" Grabbing the glass from the bar, Layla sips on her champagne.

I turn, letting her step between my legs. My hand settles low on her hip.

"Fighting over who is going to win tonight. Apparently babysitting is on the line."

Layla snorts out a laugh. "Is that what the world has come to? I'm pretty sure they used to bet that the other got to pick the next one's tattoo."

"Damn. That would've been good to see."

Being here with Layla is easy. As worried as she was about tonight, she's slipped into this new role effortlessly. I don't know if she even realizes she's doing it. The two of us move together like we've always been doing this.

If it's going to be like this for the next few weeks, it'll be the simplest thing I've ever done.

"Alright, all you lovebirds. Let's get going." Logan's voice calls out over the room.

"You ready?" Layla sucks in a deep breath.

Leaning down, I whisper in her ear, "Relax. It's going to be fine."

Her smile is tight as we head into the cozy sitting area of the main lodge. With oversized couches and an empty fireplace, I can see how inviting this space could be in the middle of winter. Perfect for curling up with someone after a day of skiing.

Someone like Layla.

Shite.

I really need to quell the thoughts racing through my brain.

This thing with Layla isn't real. And the sooner my brain gets the memo, the better.

"Does everyone know the rules of the game?" Logan asks the gathered group.

Heads nod.

"Good. You'll get one point for every right answer. We'll take turns, going back and forth. At the end, I'll announce the winner."

"Why are you announcing the winner?" Peter asks from his spot across from us.

"Because I don't trust any of you not to cheat."

"And I know you will." Gemma points at her brother. "You guys are going down."

"Is your entire family like this?" I sit on the love seat next to Layla, picking up the two whiteboards and markers.

She claps her hand on my thigh, leaving it there. "Yes."

"Not real comforting, love."

"What do you want me to say?" She rests her chin on my shoulder. Her face is close to mine. So close, I can study every detail I want without shame.

The small patch of freckles crossing the bridge of her

nose. The small dimple that comes out when she's smiling like this. Or how small flecks of green play in her eyes.

God, she really is the most fucking beautiful woman I've ever met.

"Winchesters don't go easy on each other," Layla whispers, "so we better sell this."

I don't think selling it is going to be hard at this point.

"Wait." Logan's voice breaks through the haze. "You can't be sitting next to each other. Then you'll all cheat and there's no point in playing."

"Play nice with the others." Layla presses a kiss to my cheek.

"I'll try."

Standing, I head over to sit on the chair next to Pierce and Sean.

"Try not to look so sad you're not with your girl," Pierce tells me.

"I'd rather be with her than you, you tosser."

"You wound me." He rolls his eyes at me.

"First question." Logan's voice is louder than necessary, quieting the large group. "What did you and your partner do on your first date? And I want details. Going to dinner doesn't count."

"How much detail?" Pierce asks.

"Not that much detail, darling," Charlotte calls from across the room. It has everyone breaking out into laughter.

Of course the first question is one that we wouldn't have an answer to.

Layla's blue eyes find mine across the room. She's studying me, trying to come up with something on the spot.

"Ten seconds."

Jesus. They weren't kidding around. I scrawl the first thing that pops into my head.

"And time. Everyone show your boards."

All boards are flipped. A few people get theirs wrong, but surprisingly, Layla and I match.

Picnic in the park.

Pierce eyes my board. "I didn't know you were such a romantic."

"It's because I'm not trying to woo you."

"Woo me? You big sap."

"Come off it." I shove him away from me as I wipe my board.

Layla's still smiling across the room from me. I send a wink her way, and watch a blush spread up her face. I'd love to see where else that blush would spread to.

The questions keep coming. We know some of the answers, but get others wrong. It's fast-paced and it's hard to keep track of how many points we have.

"Okay, let's wrap this up." Logan's looking flustered as Mason and Gemma are fuming at one another, bickering with each other about what the right answer is and why they should get the point.

"Final question for the women. When your partner was little, what did he want to be when he grew up?"

Layla eyes me. A coy smile plays at the corner of her mouth before she scribbles something down on her board. My answer is easy.

"Show me your answers."

James Bond.

"Fuck yeah!" I pump my fist in victory at seeing Layla's matching answer.

"How in the world did you know that?" Pierce shouts at Layla across the room.

"He owns his own security firm. C'mon, Pierce. It was

easy. Don't be a sore loser." He and Charlotte missed their answers.

"That's just mean." He's pouting in his seat.

"How do all three of you have the same answer?" Gemma points her marker at Sean, Pierce and me.

"Because he is a badass." Pierce gives me a high five.

I stride across the room, pulling Layla up and into my arms. "Who didn't want to be James Bond growing up? He always got his lady."

"Oh, am I your lady now?" She licks her lips, staring up at me.

"I believe you are."

Layla pushes me off her with a laugh. "We'll see about that."

"Okay. Does everyone have a drink so I can announce the winners?" Logan announces.

"How do you think we did?" Layla's attention is solely on me.

This is something I like about her. When she's with you, her focus is on you. It's not straying to her phone or anyone around you.

"I don't think we came in dead last."

"Nice vote of confidence you have in us, Simon."

"In third place, we have Sean and Ellie."

"Yes!" Ellie leaps into Sean's awaiting arms. "We win free babysitting!"

"You didn't win yet!" Pierce is irate as he stands up. "Who came in second?"

"Gemma and Blake." Logan clears his throat. "And the dark horse winners of tonight are Layla and Simon."

"Hell yes!" Layla wraps her arms around my neck in excitement, kicking her legs up. "I can't believe we won!"

"Bloody brilliant!" I squeeze her close to me. "You were amazing."

"Me? You were." Layla's eyes are sparkling as she pulls back.

It would be so easy to kiss her right now. I'm so caught up in her spell, I don't notice anyone else around us.

"Pretty damn good of both of us."

"Congratulations, guys." Gemma interrupts the moment, passing over the winning bottle of vodka.

"Cheers." I take it from her. "Good game."

"Worthy competition." Gemma gives me a quick side hug. "I'm glad you could make it, Simon."

"Thanks, sis." Layla gives her a quick peck on the cheek before she goes back to Blake.

"You feeling better now?" My voice is low, so only Layla can hear me.

"Maybe you did grow up to be James Bond. Pulling this off all sly and everything."

"Layla, I've got moves you've never seen."

And I plan on using every single one of them on this woman.

Chapter Twelve

LAYLA

"Erica. Where's the new shipment of accessories that came in?"

"It hasn't come yet."

"Seriously?"

Just what I need. Something else not going to plan today. With trying to do everything I can to save my store, it feels like I've been running around with even less free time than normal.

The shop has been packed today. Thankfully I have great help, but I step in when needed. Instead of spending the day working on Gemma's dress like I wanted to, I know I'll be working on it all night. That is if I can get out of whatever wedding events are tonight.

A bonfire and movie night, I think?

"Okay. Grab what we have for next week's new release and put that out. We'll have to make do."

The door to the shop swings open and just about the last person I expect to see is here. In the middle of the day.

"Simon. What are you doing here?"

On instinct, I look down at what I'm wearing. My

wide-legged, pinstripe, linen jumpsuit is perfect. Not that Simon cares what I'm wearing, but I like the reaction I get out of him when he sees me.

It's been a few days since I've seen him, when we won the newlywed game. Sure, he's been around town with Pierce and Charlotte, but my sole focus this week has been getting Gemma's dress done. I want it to be perfect before the wedding so I can enjoy the week with all the festivities.

"Bringing some guests over." He hands me a brown paper sack with the ranch's logo on it. "Brought you some lunch too."

"Really?" I take the bag and open it, inhaling the delicious scents no doubt cooked up by the ranch's chef.

"Thought you might need something." He shrugs a shoulder like this isn't a big deal. "Wasn't sure if you'd have a break today."

Except it is a big deal. No one has ever brought me lunch before. If I'm busy, I'll snack here and there, but never sit down to eat.

"Thank you, Simon." Placing a hand on his chest, I push up and drop a quick kiss on his cheek. Except he doesn't let me pull back. His warm hand comes over mine, keeping me in place.

"You deserve to have someone bring you lunch. Every woman should."

It's almost like he can read my mind. Like he's telling me that no matter what this is, fake or real, he's genuine.

But there's also something in his words like he's seen what men can be like. I don't know Simon as far as I can throw him, but there's a hurt there.

I only hope that I can show him how much he can trust me.

"Layla?" Simon dips down, bringing my focus back to him.

"Sorry. Where are these guests?" I look around him, but he's by himself.

"Charlotte and Ellie wanted to come see the store. They're grabbing a coffee with one of my guys."

"Didn't trust your men to bring them on their own?" I quirk a brow at him.

"More like those two can be a handful if they want to be," he says with a laugh.

"You wouldn't happen to be talking about us, now would you?"

The bell of the door chimes as another familiar voice rings out over the crowded store.

"Charlotte. Ellie. I'm so happy you girls wanted to stop by!" I step out of Simon's hold and wrap the two of them up in a hug.

"Were we interrupting something?" Ellie eyes me and Simon, who has now taken a step back.

"You weren't."

"Sure." Charlotte gives me a studying appraisal.

"What brings you two over?" I want to take the focus off me. And Simon. Because no matter how hard I try, he keeps pulling my attention.

"We wanted to do some shopping while we're here." Charlotte waggles her eyebrows. I know exactly what she's talking about.

"I most certainly can help you with that." I turn to find my assistant. "Hey Erica, can you watch the store while I help them?"

Her eyes are wide as she trails behind us. I forget sometimes that I'm used to being around the princesses since my cousins married them, but not everyone is.

They aren't some fairy-tale versions of princesses, but real-life working royalty. Even though Ellie stepped down from the throne, everyone still calls her Princess. It's a title that I don't think will ever go away.

"Sure thing."

"Thank you."

"Everything in here is gorgeous." Charlotte walks between racks, touching everything within reach. "I know you make the lingerie, but do you design these as well?"

"Not all of them. But I did design this." I flourish my hand in front of me.

"I love it. I'll need one of those too."

"Same." Ellie nods. "I don't know how I won't buy one of everything."

I follow them around the store, finding the right sizes and pointing out anything they might like. Their enthusiasm is why I love my job.

"I think we have one of everything." Charlotte's arms are as full as mine, loaded down with clothes and lingerie alike.

"I'll set you up in the changing suite. Head on in here. I can grab any different sizes you might need, and feel free to model if you feel comfortable."

Charlotte nods her head. "I will absolutely be modeling these for you. I can't wait to try them on."

She's giddy as she heads into her private changing room within the suite.

I hand Ellie her items. "You start trying those on and I'll grab us some wine."

"Talk about the VIP treatment."

"Anything for you two."

I run back into my studio to grab the bottle of sauvignon blanc I keep there and a few glasses.

Giggles are heard as I sit in the waiting area outside their changing rooms. I created this so friends could be together and try on lingerie in peace.

Deep-purple velvet wallpaper lines the space and heavy sconces hang on the walls, giving this room a more intimate feel.

"How's it looking in there?"

I pour us each a glass before opening up the bag Simon brought for me. A caprese sandwich. I scarf down as much of it as I can while the two of them are trying on clothes. With each new piece, they come out and show me. Their beaming smiles are why I love doing this and designing clothes.

"Layla. You designed this?" Charlotte comes out of the dressing room in my newest set designed for the summer. The bra is bright purple with black stitching used at the seams to make it pop. The underwear match perfectly.

The robe that completes the set is made of the same silky purple fabric. And it looks absolutely stunning on Charlotte with her olive skin and dark hair.

"It's part of my newest collection."

Her mouth drops. "This is fab. I didn't know you could do all of this. You are seriously talented."

"She really is." Ellie steps out of her room with a more conservative, yet still sexy, one-piece bodysuit. Made out of hot-pink lace, it matches Ellie's hair perfectly. "Sean is going to lose his mind when he sees this."

I drop my sandwich and grab the wine glasses. Each take their proffered glass.

"Cheers, ladies. I'm so happy you stopped by."

"Best way to spend the afternoon," Ellie says.

"You know, maybe you can show some of this off to your fiancé." Charlotte laughs, sipping on the wine I gave her.

"Charlotte, please." Ellie waves her off. "You know he's seen all of it."

"Ellie!" My gaze snaps back to hers.

"What? Don't tell me you aren't designing all this lingerie with him in mind."

Ellie fingers the hot-pink, sheer lace bodysuit. "How can he possibly contain himself to not rip this off you?"

I laugh. "He knows he's a dead man if he does. You don't destroy handmade lingerie."

"So I should tell Sean to handle with care?"

I wince. "What you two do on your own time, I don't want to know."

"It would be a travesty if you couldn't wear that again," Charlotte points out. "I'm thinking I might need to get one too."

I love how comfortable these two women are. Seeing how excited they are and how beautiful they feel is the reason I started this company in the first place. I knew it wouldn't be easy, but I love seeing strong, confident women comfortable in their own skin, no matter their size.

"Where do you get your inspiration, Layla?" Charlotte asks. She's standing on the pedestal in front of the three-way mirror, admiring what she's wearing.

"Everywhere." I kick my shoes off and rest my feet on the small couch back here. This room really is the best. "I'll see flowers out on a hike and want to incorporate them into pieces. I love bright colors."

"You really do." Ellie runs a hand over the soft material of her bodysuit. "God, I want this in every color."

"I know a girl." I throw a wink her way.

"If you make more of these, I'm snatching every one of them up."

"That makes two of us." Charlotte spins around and walks my way. "Now, we want all the gossip on this hot fiancé of yours."

I gulp down my wine. "You know him just as well as I do."

Charlotte waves me off. Ellie drops down onto the floor next to her. "He's Pierce's mate. I want the good stuff."

"Like what?"

Charlotte leans in close, her eyes sparkling. I know what ever question comes next, the answer will be a lie.

"How is he in bed?"

I can't say I haven't pictured it. Because the smooth cadence of Simon's voice has me needing my vibrator.

"Would you look at that blush!" Ellie laughs. "Simon knows how to please our girl."

"Oh my God." My face is hot from embarrassment now. "I can't believe we're having this conversation."

"You make this beautiful lingerie, but talking about your fiancé in bed makes you blush?"

More because I'm lying, but I don't tell them that.

"Whatever happened to 'don't kiss and tell'?"

"Not between friends." Ellie waves me off.

"Let's just say…it's the best I've ever had."

"I knew it!" Charlotte pours herself a bit more wine. "How can you stand being away from him all the time?"

"Video chats. Lots of them." I sip my wine.

"I'm sure you drive him wild, modeling all of these." Ellie motions to the lingerie hanging in the room.

"If you only knew."

There's a knock on the door.

"I'll grab it."

One of Simon's men is at the door. "I was told we need to be back at the ranch."

"We'll be ready shortly."

I close the door and turn back to Ellie and Charlotte. "Time to get going."

"I've got a call to take for the foundation." Ellie looks upset. "I'm sorry to cut the afternoon short."

"That means you get to come back."

"And buy more of everything."

"Your money is no good here."

They both shake their heads at me. "No. We're paying you for all of this. It will be money well spent."

"Fine," I relent, begrudgingly. "I'll meet you outside."

Giving them privacy, I head back into the shop to find Simon.

"Everything go well?" He's waiting by the door to my studio.

"Went great."

He's standing at attention, ready to pounce if a need arises. If only I could pounce on him and see what he's really like in bed.

"Don't worry, Simon. We left some lingerie for her too." Charlotte's smile is wicked as she leaves the dressing room. She and Ellie are laughing as they take everything to the front to check out.

My face runs hot. Simon doesn't let anything show on his, but I can see the slight widening of his eyes and the way his eyes dip lower.

I'd kill for him to see me in one of my pieces. To feel his hands on my skin. Feel that stubble of his against my inner thighs.

"I'll see you tonight?" Simon drops close to my ear.

Does he know how much he affects me?

"You will."

Charlotte and Ellie wave as they leave the store, Simon and his guys with them.

I only hope the guilt of lying to everyone will have subsided by then. But if I get to keep this feeling that I've had today with these beautiful women?

It'll be worth it.

Chapter Thirteen

SIMON

"Wow. This place looks amazing."

"You've got that right." Layla's eyes are taking everything in.

Gemma went above and beyond for tonight's event. Wanting to include all the children that are visiting for her wedding, she set up a bonfire and movie night.

Huge picnic blankets and pillows are set up in front of a screen playing some animated movie for the kids. A long table is spread out next to the bonfire with marshmallows and chocolate for making s'mores.

Once the kids go to bed, there's nothing I want more than to snuggle up with Layla, eating s'mores and watching a movie under the stars.

For show, of course.

"Finally. Adults!" Peter comes over to us with his partner, Nash.

"You do know there are adults here, right?" Layla gives her brother a hug.

"They're all dealing with their children."

"Good to know where you stand on having kids." Nash laughs.

"I just can't take the sing-alongs. A song about dancing fish is going to be stuck in my head on repeat."

"You have something against this song?" Sean ambles over to our small group, grabbing a marshmallow and popping it in his mouth.

"Yes," Peter is quick to answer.

"You know, you could just leave," Sean laughs.

"No way. I made hot chocolate vodkas for us. I want to test them out."

"I'm sure they'll be great, Peter." Nash drops a kiss on his temple.

"If they're anything like that vodka we had the other night, I'll try anything," I tell him.

"Glad you two enjoyed it. Maybe I'll have to send some with Layla the next time she visits."

"You will," I tell him.

It's already hard thinking about this thing being over. Fuck. I shouldn't be so enthralled with Layla. We're only here for a few more weeks. But damn if I haven't imagined feeling those curves of hers without any clothes. Or what it'd be like to slide into her tight, wet heat.

I shift my pants, trying to hide what this woman is doing to me.

"You doing okay over here, mate?" Sean moves over beside me and hands me a drink.

"Doing great." I clink my bottle against his. "Cheers."

"I'm sure you are. Now that you actually get to spend time with your fiancée."

"Be grateful you don't have to do long-distance."

"Fecking hell, I couldn't do a day away from Ellie."

Sean and Ellie are so sickeningly in love, it normally

would bother me. But not tonight. Tonight it's easier to handle because I have Layla on my arm.

"We make do."

"You're a better man than I am."

"Drinking on the job?" Mason asks.

"I have tomorrow off."

"Good man. Don't want you hungover on the job."

"That's Pierce's job."

"What's my job?" Pierce asks, joining our small group.

Layla and Charlotte have gone to corral the younger kids as the movie nears the end. Whines are heard about not wanting to go to bed.

My eyes keep sweeping the area. I know I'm not on duty tonight, but it's a force of habit. Always on alert.

"Tattooing hungover," Sean tells him.

He shakes his head. "Not in our shop." Pierce laughs. "But maybe when you and Layla come next time I might. When is your girl going to come visit us in London?"

Your girl.

Fuck, I wish that statement were true. As if a magnet to her, my eyes land on her immediately. No matter where she is, I can find her in a moment.

Layla has Mary in her arms, rocking her gently. If that isn't a sight to behold.

I've never wanted kids. Being an only child and growing up how I did, it was never something I wanted. Seeing Layla now?

I could entertain that idea with her.

"Hopefully I'll get her there sooner rather than later. Otherwise I'm flying back here."

The woman in question wanders in our direction. "You boys are needed for bedtime."

Layla hands off the child in her arms to Pierce as they head toward the lodge.

"Having fun with your mates?" Her smile is bright.

"Listen to you, you cheeky little shit."

"What can I say? My British fiancé is rubbing off on me."

Grabbing a roasting stick, Layla hands one to me. "Dessert and then would you care to join me for our movie?"

They could play that blasted kids' movie again and I'd sit through it if I got to spend time with Layla.

"Only because of the s'mores."

"Of course."

I watch Layla as she makes hers, and I step in close beside her. Everything this woman does is mesmerizing. I shouldn't be so taken with her—she's roasting a fucking marshmallow—but everything she does is sensual.

"Are you not making yours?"

Layla is holding a perfectly crisped marshmallow and mine is still white.

"Figured I should have a taste of yours. See how to cook it."

Quirking a brow at me, Layla makes her s'more. "Try it."

She holds her hand out to me to take it from her, but I don't. Instead, wrapping my fingers around her wrist, I bring the dessert to my mouth and take a bite.

Her eyes darken as they dip to my mouth.

"You've got a little..." Layla's finger brushes over my mouth, coming back with marshmallow on it. I watch as she sucks her finger into her mouth.

Holy shit.

The thought of her doing that to me—to my dick—slams into my brain. This girl is doing everything in her power to drive me crazy.

How the hell am I not supposed to fall for my fake

fiancée when she's looking at me like she wants to devour me?

"Would you two get a room?"

"Oh goodie. Pierce is back."

Layla takes a step away from me, that blush creeping up into her cheeks.

"I came to tell you it's time for the movie."

"We'll be right there."

Layla busies herself getting desserts while I grab a few of the hot chocolates for us. By the time we get over to where the movie is playing, all the spots are taken except one in the middle.

Great.

"I guess this for us."

I drop down, pulling her next to me. The oversized jumper she's wearing slips down her shoulder. All I want to do is kiss her there. Do a lot more.

Christ. Now every single thought of mine is dirty.

What is this woman doing to me?

An old western movie starts playing, nothing I've seen before. The movie drones on, barely holding my attention.

Until a wedding scene comes on. Glasses clink as the couple kisses on-screen. Around us, a glass clinks.

"Kiss, kiss!" someone shouts.

"Isn't that only at the reception?" Gemma laughs, turning from her spot at the front to look at the rest of us.

"It'd be bad luck if we didn't." Blake waggles his brows at her.

"If we have to, everyone has to. I don't like being the center of attention."

"Oh shit," Layla mutters next to me.

We're slap bang in the middle of everyone. There's no way we can get out of this.

Layla shifts, turning to face me. She looks nervous. It feels like every set of eyes is on us.

Cupping her jaw, my thumb caresses her cheek. Her tongue darts out to wet her lips. Shite, I don't think I can wait any longer.

Dipping down, her eyes flutter closed as I close my lips over hers.

Holy fuck. She tastes like chocolate and marshmallows. I glide my tongue along the seam of her mouth, and she opens on a gasp.

My hands move around her waist and haul her closer to me. Layla's tongue tangles with mine in the most delicious of ways.

This woman knows exactly what she wants and she's taking it.

It's hot as hell as her tongue moves with mine. I eat up the moans that slip through as she fists her hands in my shirt, keeping me locked in place.

I'm impossibly hard. From a kiss. When was the last time that happened?

I don't know how much time has passed before Layla pulls back. She looks drunk off our kiss.

The sounds of the movie filter through as I glance around us. It's dark enough that no one is paying us any attention.

Because if they were, they'd see how this woman just rocked my fucking world.

The movie ends, but I haven't paid attention to a minute of it since the wedding scene. The sole focus of my thoughts has been Layla.

Layla stands, helping Gemma collect the blankets. Taking a breath of Layla-free air, my mind starts to settle.

No matter how good that kiss was, this is all a ruse. Something to get her ex off her back.

Maybe if I tell myself that, I'll start to believe it.

"You two need a ride back into town?" Mason asks, startling me from my thoughts.

"Simon's staying here at the ranch," Layla is quick to point out.

"I thought you had tomorrow off?" Mason asks. "I just assumed you'd need a ride since I brought you here, Layla."

Damn him for being so on top of it.

"You're right, I do," Layla sighs.

"Then you need a lift?" He looks between the two of us. "I'm assuming you're staying at Layla's."

"I've got her. I'll take her home," I tell him.

"You will?" Layla's face doesn't give anything away.

"Of course, love."

Shite. Maybe I can sneak back to the ranch after I drop her off. Because there is no way that my self-control can take sleeping in the same room as her.

Because after one kiss, I want more. And after that one fake kiss?

I can't imagine what the real thing will be like with Layla.

Chapter Fourteen

LAYLA

"Are you sure about this? I can head back and stay at the lodge."

Unlocking the front door, I let Simon in before me.

"It's fine. I don't want anyone asking any questions."

Because after that heated kiss, anything less than Simon coming home with me would draw too many eyes.

"Who's this?"

"She hates most people."

Luna circles his feet, nipping at his shoelaces.

"Animals love me." Simon bends down, picking her up.

"Careful!" I lurch toward them, not wanting her to scratch at him.

"What's her name?" Simon pays no attention to me, nuzzling into Luna's soft fur.

"Luna."

She lets out a contented meow as Simon continues petting her.

"She hates people?" He turns a raised brow to me.

"Not you apparently." Luna purrs, cuddling in closer to Simon.

Even my cat likes Simon. Is there anyone that doesn't fall for his charm?

"I'm going to go get cleaned up."

"Okay." Simon is still loving on Luna, my cat eating it up like she's deprived for attention. "I'll sleep out on the couch."

"Are you sure?"

Simon eyes the small sectional that takes up most of the living room. "I'm sure."

I'm quick in the bathroom, not wanting Simon to think I'm avoiding him. Grabbing the robe from the back of the door, I slip out of my clothes and pull the satin material closed before opening the door.

Simon is folding his jeans, setting them on the coffee table. In only a T-shirt and boxers, he has thrown my mind into overdrive.

"Layla."

My eyes snap up to meet his. The smile on his face tells me he caught me staring.

"Yeah?"

"What do you think about making the most of this little arrangement?"

"Meaning…"

I know exactly what he means. I want him to spell it out for me.

"After that kiss tonight?" He waves a finger between the two of us. "There's something here. Might as well enjoy each other's company while we're together."

Simon grabs the neck of his T-shirt and pulls it over his head, revealing a long line of delicious abs. He's cut, but not overly bulky.

"Umm…" I lick my lips, trying to find the words to answer him.

"Your decision, Layla." Simon closes the distance

between us, pressing a warm kiss to the corner of my mouth before retreating.

"Let me know if you need anything." My voice is breathy.

"Thanks, love."

I sneak into my room, trying to close out all the unwanted thoughts of the man in the next room.

No matter what I do, I can't get comfortable. Sleep is elusive.

Simon is consuming my every thought.

This situation is already messy as it is. Adding sex to the mix would only make it that much more complicated.

This isn't like me. I make decisions all damn day for a living. So why am I not sharing a bed right now with the sexiest man I've ever met?

And that kiss?

My mind keeps drifting back to that kiss. It was so damn good, it's all I can think about. The way it caused my toes to curl and heat to flood my veins. I moved through the rest of the evening in a lust-filled fog. Sitting next to him, curled up watching the movie, was a test of my patience.

Every soft caress of his fingers against my skin had me ready to jump his bones.

And now I let him sleep on the couch?

What an idiot.

The door to my room creaks open.

"Layla?" Simon's voice is a whisper. I suck in a breath.

What's he doing in here?

The streetlights cast him in a faint glow. The bed shifts as he sits down next to me.

"Are you awake?"

His hand ghosts over my shoulder as I sit up.

"What are you doing?" I hiss, leaning over and turning on the lamp.

"You left this on my chest." Simon holds up a mint-green thong. "I thought it was your way of telling me to come in here."

"What?" I snatch them from his hold, embarrassment snaking through me. "God damn it, Luna."

"Wait, your cat did this?" Simon looks horrified.

"She loves unmentionables. I forgot to put them away."

"I feel like a fucking arse." Simon scrubs a hand down his face and heads to the door. "I'm just going to go find a cave to hide in for the next few weeks and pretend this didn't happen."

Oh God. Of all the turns this night could have taken, this isn't what I thought would happen. My cat has more balls than I do.

I've been trying to resist this man since he showed up in town and came to my rescue. And after that kiss tonight?

I was ready to pull out my vibrator and take care of my own needs. Like I've been doing for the last however many years.

Except Simon is here. Here and willing.

Why not take advantage of what my fake fiancé is offering?

"Wait." I throw back the duvet and get out of bed.

Simon stops, not turning around. His back muscles flex as I get closer.

"Simon, I…"

Now that the moment is here, words are escaping me.

"Yeah?"

I press a kiss to the middle of his back. "I want this. I want you."

Chapter Fifteen

"**I** want this. I want you."

Fucking finally.

"Yeah?" I turn, wrapping an arm around Layla's waist and pulling her in close. The ruby-red robe she's wearing is short, giving me a glimpse of those long legs beneath.

"Like you said, might as well make the most of this arrangement."

Sweeping the hair back from her neck, I take what I want. What she's finally giving to me.

Her pulse is firing under my lips as I suck on the warm skin. Fuck, she tastes delicious.

Her hands hold me to her as I snake one of my hands around her stomach, finding the sash on the robe to untie.

The soft material slips off her. And fuck me. Layla's in a matching top and underwear set. Made of sheer fabric, the light-pink material is laced with what looks to be tiny blue flowers.

"Did you make this?" I trace a finger over the camisole, watching goose pimples erupt on her chest.

Her nipples are two hard points.

"I did."

"I want to rip this off you," I growl. I want this woman to be naked so I can feast on every inch of her body.

"Do that and this will be over real fast."

"Oh yeah?" I slide a finger under the strap, pulling it down over her shoulder.

"Handmade lingerie is not something that I want to see torn to shreds."

"Then how about seeing it on the floor?" I spin her, pulling her flush against me. My dick is aching, crying out to get inside this woman. "I wouldn't want to ruin this masterpiece."

I pull the top up and over her head. Pressing kisses to her shoulder, I trail my fingers up her arms.

I want nothing more than to throw her down on the bed and see her spread out before me. To taste more of her. But with the way she's arching into my touch, I want to draw out every bit of her pleasure.

I drag my fingers over her shoulder, trailing a path between her cleavage.

"Simon," Layla whimpers.

"Yes, love?"

"Touch me."

I smile into her neck, nipping on the soft skin there.

"I believe I am."

"You know what I mean." She wiggles her hips against me and fuck if that doesn't make my cock harder.

"How about this?"

I dip my hand underneath the soft fabric of the thong she's wearing and find her dripping for me. Parting her pussy, I find her clit.

"Yes!" Layla grabs my arm, holding me in place. "Keep doing that."

"You want to come on my fingers?" I keep my touch light, swirling soft circles over her tight bundle of nerves. She's grinding down onto my hand as I slip a finger inside of her.

"I want you to make me come."

"That I can do."

Withdrawing my hand, I spin Layla in my arms and take her mouth in a punishing kiss. I swallow every moan as she clings to me.

She presses herself farther into me, letting me feel all of that skin. I nip and suck at her lips, getting lost in her.

Every time her tongue touches mine, it's like a line directly to my cock. I've never been so painfully hard in my life.

Breaking the kiss, I step us closer to the bed.

"Lie down."

Smiling, Layla complies.

"Damn, Layla."

I palm my cock, willing him to behave because the last thing I want to do is come before I'm inside this woman. Before I enjoy her body.

Because what a body it is. Dusty-pink nipples are tight. A damp patch on her thong shows how turned on she is. And those legs—I can't wait to feel them wrapped around me.

"You are without a doubt the sexiest woman on the planet."

My eyes are greedy, drinking in every bit of her. Shucking off my boxers, I crawl to her.

"Looks like someone is ready for me." I drag a finger over the wet material.

"I want your mouth on my pussy."

I love the confidence in Layla's voice. She knows exactly what she wants and asks for it.

Dragging my tongue over the material, I savor her taste. I want more.

Hooking a finger through the material, I drag it down her legs and toss it behind me. A small line of curls points directly to where I want to be.

I press featherlight kisses up her leg, getting closer and closer to the promised land.

"You are such a tease." Layla is squirming beneath me.

"And someone is impatient." I pause, just long enough for Layla to grab my bicep and pull me so my face is level with hers.

"What can I say? You aren't the only one who wanted this to happen."

"Oh yeah?"

This time, I sink a finger inside her, curling it just so, and she cries out in pleasure.

"Do that again."

Her nails sink into my back. It's the tiniest bit of pain mixed with pleasure as Layla rocks into my touch.

She's a writhing mess beneath me as I push two fingers inside her.

"Oh Simon. Yes, yes, yes!"

A blush blooms across her chest as she rides my hand. I draw one tight nipple into my mouth, swirling my tongue around it.

That pushes her over the edge. Her pussy clamps down on my fingers as she rides out the tidal wave of her orgasm.

I can't understand a single word of what she's saying as she holds on to me. Fuck. It's the single hottest thing I've seen in my life watching Layla come undone like this.

"Holy shit."

"Feel good?"

Her eyes peep open as I pull out, sucking my fingers into my mouth to taste her release.

"Damn, you taste good, Layla."

Wrapping her hands around my neck, Layla pulls me down for a heated kiss. Our tongues tangle as she moans into my mouth.

I love the sounds she's making.

"Got a condom?" she asks, pulling back.

"Hang on." I dart out to the living room, grabbing a condom from my wallet. When I come back, Layla hasn't moved.

Layla's eyes are on me as I tear open the foil pouch.

"Wait."

Getting onto her hands and knees, she crawls toward me, taking my dick in hand. She gives me a solid stroke before licking the leaking head.

"Fuck."

"So good," she hums around me.

"I've imagined you doing this."

"Oh yeah?" She pulls off me with a pop, continuing to stroke me.

Fisting my hands in her hair, I guide her mouth back. She opens wide, sucking me to the back of her throat.

"When you sucked your finger in your mouth tonight? I imagined it was my dick."

The way she hums and vibrates around me has heat racing down my spine. I'm way too close to coming. And I won't do it down her throat for the first time.

"On your back."

Layla wipes the corner of her mouth before obeying me. I take back my earlier statement. Watching her like this is the hottest fucking thing ever.

Layla's watching intently as I roll the condom over my cock.

"I can't wait to feel you inside me."

I squeeze myself, trying to stave off my impending

release. This woman drives me absolutely crazy.

Settling myself over her, I line myself up and start to slide in. I can feel her pulsing still from her orgasm.

I thrust my hips, testing her out, slipping in just a little more.

"I want it all." Layla wraps her legs around me, digging her heels into my arse and pulling me all the way in.

"Fuck!"

Fuck, does that ever feel good.

Layla echoes my thoughts. "Simon. That feels amazing."

She rocks her hips, bringing me that much deeper inside of her. I pump my hips, relishing each squeeze as I dive back into her warmth.

Each brush of her nipples against my chest quickens my pace. My lips suck on the pulse pounding in her neck.

Everything about this moment is charged.

"I'm coming!" Layla shouts. Her squeezing around me tips me over the edge.

"Fuck," I bite out on a growl, emptying myself into the condom. "Fuuuuck."

I collapse onto my arms, not putting my full weight onto Layla.

"That was…" Layla's hand cups my chin, bringing my gaze to hers.

"That was what?" I ask, dropping my forehead to hers.

"Pretty damn incredible."

I take a quick kiss before pulling out of her and tying off the condom and dropping it onto the floor. Layla slides under the duvet, and I move in next to her.

"Tomorrow morning…" I cup Layla's cheek, dragging my thumb over her lips. Her eyes are hazy with lust.

"Yeah?" She leans into my touch.

"Remind me to thank your cat."

Chapter Sixteen

SIMON

"Mm, morning, love." I stretch out, my muscles sore after a long night with Layla. We spent most of the night tangled up in her sheets.

Turning to face the other side of the bed, I'm met with a pair of glowing yellow eyes. Luna purrs as I scratch between her ears.

"I guess I should be thanking you, you little menace."

Because without this interfering feline, I don't think I'd be waking up as satisfied as I am. Everything about last night was perfect.

Every time I'm around Layla, I get this same feeling. Like there is no other woman in the world that I need. It's something I've never felt before.

Work has always come first for me. Attachments just make my job harder when I'm gone for long stretches of time.

Layla is an attachment I wouldn't mind making more permanent.

Leaving Luna to herself, I put on my boxers and tread out to the kitchen. The small apartment is empty. Coffee is brewing with a mug sitting next to the machine with a note.

Downstairs working. Didn't want to wake you <3

I pour myself a quick cup before swallowing it down and heading to find Layla. The whir of a machine echoes in the empty stairwell. Pushing open her workroom door, my breath catches. Layla looks stunning.

All that blonde hair—that I loved seeing spread out on her pillow last night—is piled on top of her head. She's wearing a black bralette with sage green shorts and a matching robe.

I watch her as she works, feeding a dark-green fabric through the machine. I've never seen someone so focused on what they're doing.

I knock once on the door, and Layla jumps.

"Morning, love."

"You're awake."

"How long was I out?" I walk over to her, pulling her into my arms.

"I woke up early."

"And you didn't wake me up?" I nuzzle into her neck. She smells like sex and that perfume she wears that drives me absolutely wild. "Didn't want another round this morning?"

"If I thought you could handle it…"

"Cheeky little shit." I tickle her side as she squirms in my arms.

"Stop it, Simon!" She laughs, trying to get away from me.

"Take it back."

"Fine! Fine! I couldn't handle it. Your penis broke me."

"It broke you?" That gets me to stop. I feel like a caveman wanting to beat my chest in pride.

Layla leans back, the front of her robe falling to the side. It causes me to lose focus. Her nipples are hard through her bra, and it makes me want to suck them into my mouth.

"You'd like to think it did, wouldn't you?" A playful smile crosses her face. "I would not mind doing more of last night."

"Good." I trail a path of kisses up her neck. "Because I have not had my fill of you."

I don't know if I ever will.

There's something about Layla that draws me to her. There's a quiet strength to her that I think most people don't realize. I don't know if it's because of her divorce, but it is clear she doesn't want to rely on anyone.

I want to be that person for her. Even though my time here is limited, I want her to be able to depend on me. To let me help her carry her load from time to time. She does so much for everyone around her, that I want to help her anyway I can.

God knows she needs it with the people in this town.

"You have to stop doing that," Layla moans, tilting her head to the side.

"Why's that, love?" I pull her closer to me, letting her feel exactly what she's doing to me.

"Because we can't have sex down here."

The table with her sewing machine is clean except for the fabric she is currently sewing.

"I don't know. This looks fairly sturdy to me."

Layla pushes me off her. "You want a needle in the ass?"

"Are you serious?" A shudder racks my body.

"It wouldn't be fun."

"Does that mean you've had a needle in your arse?"

"No. But I don't want to try and find one to see what it feels like." Layla sets what she's working on to the side. "So why don't we go back upstairs and you can have your way with me there?"

"I have a question for you first."

Layla crosses one leg over the other. "Yes?"

"Can I take you out?"

"What, like a date?"

"Typically when a man takes a woman out, yes, that would mean a date."

She looks confused. "But we've already gone out on a date."

"Does it really count when we did it to be seen?"

Nerves coil in my gut. *Why am I so nervous about her answer?*

"A real date then?"

"A novel idea when I've already seen you naked, but yes."

"Will it involve more of what we did last night?"

I laugh. "I don't really want to be arrested for indecent exposure, love."

"Might throw a wrench into my plans of being a Dixonite of good moral standing."

"Yes, love, they wouldn't want to see all of you out like that." I drag a finger down her chest. "Me on the other hand? I'm ready to see more."

"Maybe I should make you wait until our date then."

"Is that a yes?"

Layla closes the distance between us, sealing her lips

over mine. She tastes like mint and coffee. I lick the seam of her lips, easily being granted entry.

It's a slow kiss—lazy like the morning we're having. Her hands drift up and down my chest, setting my skin on fire. I can't get enough. I drink in everything she pours into this kiss. I could do this for hours and not get tired.

All I want is Layla. And for now, I'll take her anyway I can have her.

She breaks the kiss first.

I smile against her lips. "I'll take that as a yes."

Chapter Seventeen

SIMON

"**D**oes this actually count as work?" Pierce asks me, lacing up his hiking boots. "Because it doesn't seem like real work to me.

"Making sure you don't fall down the side of a mountain without someone taking your photo? That's a job unto itself."

"Funny." Pierce flips me off.

As far as work goes, it's been smooth sailing. I don't know if it's because they've visited family here in the past —before I worked for them—or that the town isn't interested in royals, but it's been easy days watching the property.

And getting to spend as much time as I can with Layla.

"You ready?" Pierce asks me.

"I've been waiting on you."

With the kids down for an afternoon nap, Pierce and Charlotte wanted to get out and explore. Gramps is watching the kids, should they wake up, which means I'm on hiking duty with these two.

Not that it's a hardship.

Following them out of their cabin, they set an easy pace up the trail. Seeing as how we're staying mostly on the property, I'm not worried about running into stray paparazzi. They're too soft for these trails.

Pierce and Charlotte are holding hands, walking close together. I let my thoughts drift to Layla.

I'm so fucking happy that I bumped into her that day in the barn. I don't know if we would be together like we are now if we hadn't.

That woman is consuming my every thought. I've never met anyone like her. She's sexy. Confident. Strong.

And the way she shows off that lingerie?

Fuck. I have to adjust myself so I'm not rock-hard in my shorts.

Because Layla has that effect on me.

She's sucked me into her world. I don't care that the relationship is "fake."

What we did together at her place was anything but fake.

I'll take this woman any way I can have her.

For someone that's been all about work the last few years, it should scare me how easily I want to dive into this thing with her. My job has been my life. With running my security firm, it is convenient to give women the excuse that I don't have time for dating. I never lead them on because I don't want to hurt them.

I saw enough of that with my mom. I didn't want to be another guy that treats them like shite.

What if I get hurt in the line of duty?

It could happen, so it made it easier to not date. The reason I kept giving myself as to why I never made the time for anyone. A way to not get close.

Rarely—very rarely—does anything happen in my line

of work. And why would it when we're the only three hiking out here?

I'm thankful for that. But it's always been the reason I don't want to settle down.

Except now. Maybe I was holding out for the right person.

Could that be Layla?

It was supposed to be fake, yet here we are. Having our first real date.

And I can't fucking wait.

As we leave the ranch's property, the trees become more sparse. The sun bakes my skin as sweat clings to me.

This is something I wouldn't mind doing with Layla.

A hike? A good fuck.

Anything to get to spend the day together.

Pierce and Charlotte stop at the trailhead, where it cuts to the right.

"You still with us?" Pierce asks, chucking a water bottle at me.

"Fuck off."

"I figured you couldn't hack it, city boy."

I roll my eyes at him. "Please. I totally can."

"You two don't need to get into a pissing match about it." Charlotte wraps her arms around Pierce, tugging him into her side. "I don't need either one of you injured because your egos can't handle not winning."

"That's sweet of you, Charlotte," I tell her, "wanting to protect Pierce from losing."

"Oy!" he chirps.

"Stop it. Both of you." She sounds exasperated, but a smile is stretched across her face.

It's always like this with Pierce. It's why he's one of my best mates. And why I take these jobs with them whenever needed.

It's then I notice a couple of hikers walking over to us. I can't see their eyes behind their sunglasses, but they're trading whispers as they approach us.

"Hi. Can I ask what you're doing?"

The couple looks at me like I've lost my mind. I hold off the people from getting closer. They stop short, like I came at them with a pistol drawn.

"Sorry. You're the first people we've seen in a long time, and we were hoping you could take our picture."

They're looking at the two people behind me with no recognition. Deciding they aren't actually a threat, I go for their phone but Charlotte pushes me out of the way.

"Sorry about him. I would love to take your picture." Charlotte is beaming as she takes their phone and starts snapping away.

"They have no fucking clue she's a princess, do they?" I whisper to Pierce. Charlotte is pointing out different spots for them to pose for a picture.

It's picturesque. Everything about it from the trees to the mountains. It's different from London, but I still enjoy being out in nature.

"She loves it. Getting to talk to people without any expectation. She's made for this." Pierce is beaming at his wife as she waves the hikers off.

"They were lovely." Charlotte holds a hand out to grab the water bottle from Pierce. "In town from California to see the Tetons for the first time. Staying in Jackson since the ranch is closed."

"Is that all?" Pierce asks, dropping a kiss on her head.

"Told them a few recommendations in town. Wouldn't be surprised if we see them at The Tipsy Cocktail tonight."

"You're on your own there," I tell them.

"You were about ready to throw them down." Pierce's laughter echoes around the trees as he turns to face me.

"I was not." My senses are on high alert. You always have to be in this business, but I didn't expect anything out here. I expel a breath, trying to rid myself of the nerves of this job.

"Glad we're putting you to work." Pierce claps me on the shoulder.

"Shove off." I brush him off.

"Alright boys. Let's finish our hike. We need to make sure we're back in time for the kids."

"And your big date." Pierce gives me a playful punch on the shoulder before following after Charlotte.

That puts a smile on my face as I head off after them.

It's not hard to mind the job when I get to clock out and head out with Layla.

I can't fucking wait to spend my evening with her. And if I'm lucky, spend all night buried inside her.

Chapter Eighteen

LAYLA

"I promise, I'll be over tomorrow with your dress."

"How does it look?" Gemma asks me over speakerphone. It's set on my dresser while I put the finishing touches on my makeup and outfit for my first date with Simon.

Well, first *real* date I should say.

"You need me to tell you it looks gorgeous? Because it does."

I tie my T-shirt, showing off a sliver of skin on my stomach. I love the way it drives Simon wild.

He was vague about what we were doing tonight, but said casual. With a pair of leggings and tennis shoes, I think my outfit fits the bill.

"I can't believe my dress is done. It makes it real."

"More real than the month-long celebration we've been having?"

Gemma laughs. "The dress is tangible though. Something I know you've been working on for so long, that it being finished means the wedding is around the corner."

"I'm just glad I don't have to have the conversation

with you about what to expect on your wedding night anymore." I snicker.

"Layla!"

I can only imagine the look of horror on my sister's face.

"I said I don't have to. Calm down, sis. Sheesh, you're acting like you're not getting any."

"I'm going to hang up on you."

"Listen, you enjoy your night with Blake. I've got a hot Brit waiting for me."

We say goodbye and I do one more spin in front of the mirror.

Every minute I haven't been working on Gemma's dress or in the store, I've been with Simon.

And every day that inches closer to the wedding is also that much closer to when Simon will leave.

Once he does? My fate will be decided.

I only hope that what we've done will be good enough for this town.

I can't think about that now. Not tonight. I want to enjoy my time with Simon.

The buzzer to the downstairs door goes off. Sticking my phone in my leggings pocket, I bounce down the stairs and throw the door open.

Simon makes my skin prickle with awareness. Dressed in a black T-shirt, jacket, and joggers, he's as casual as I am. A blanket and small cooler sit on the ground at his feet. I was busy working most of the day, mailing off more packages to Bri who's buying everything I share with her. Even then, it surprised me how much I missed Simon.

"Looks like what they say is true."

"Oh yeah?" Simon pushes his sunglasses up, showing me those forest-green eyes of his. "What do they say, love?"

"That married couples start acting alike. I guess that means dressing alike too."

"Good thing you're my fiancée then." He leans down, giving me a soft kiss on the lips. "I've got something for you."

He hands me a small bag.

"What's this?"

"Open it and find out."

I give him a side-eye as I pull out the tissue paper. My breath catches in my throat as I pull out a heart made of spools of thread.

"You said roses aren't your thing."

"Simon…this is… Wow."

Brad always brought me roses. No matter how many times I told him I didn't like them, he never listened. One comment to Simon and he brings me something that shows more care and thought than my ex-husband ever showed me.

"You like it?"

I crush my lips to his, pouring everything into it. "I love it."

"If you're ever in a bind and need more thread, you can always tap into it."

I shake my head. "Never." I set it on the small table in the entryway. I don't know what the future holds for me, but I'll always cherish this.

"Now, Miss Winchester. Ready for our date?"

Simon picks up the blanket and cooler. Linking my hand in his, I fall into step with him. "Where are we going?"

"A local band is playing at the town square tonight. Perfect for a few drinks."

"A picnic in the park?" We cross the street.

"Why not make it real?" Simon grins down at me. "And look at that? We're already here."

"I hope that travel time doesn't cut into our date."

Simon spreads the blanket out near the back of the square. A small stage is set up across from us. Families and couples are clustered near the band. Food trucks line one side with tables on the other.

"It only means that we get more time after the date."

Simon drops down onto the blanket, pulling me between his legs. Back in this corner by the trees, it's like we're in our own little world.

I grab the six-pack out of the cooler and hand a drink to Simon before cracking mine open.

"To us."

"To us," he echoes.

I take an ice-cold sip of The Clara. A light breeze blows through the square as the band starts tinkering with their instruments.

"Is this your perfect date night then?"

"Being with you? Yes."

"Not what I meant, but a very good answer."

I snuggle into his hold. It's so easy being with Simon. I don't know if it was ever this easy with Brad. Simon has slotted himself so perfectly into my life, it's hard to remember a time when he wasn't here.

"Layla. How nice to see you out." Mrs. Bush is standing in front of us, a clipboard in hand.

"Just enjoying a nice evening in town."

"I'm sure." She gives us both a stern eye, jotting something on her board before moving on. She yells at two kids climbing a tree.

"She's terrible," Simon whispers to me.

"She really is."

I hate that she's the one who holds my fate in her hands. If it were anyone else, this would be a nonissue.

Except I can't say I'm upset at the results. I'm enjoying every second of this time I get to spend with my hot British fiancé.

An electric guitar cuts through the noise of the square like a tornado siren.

"Fucking hell. What is that noise?" Simon covers both of his ears.

The band starts playing an alt-rock song that has everyone in the crowd struggling with the sudden noise.

"So this is the kind of music you like?" I wince as a screech from one of the instruments blasts through the speakers.

"I like good music."

The instruments quiet as the lead singer starts in on a song I don't recognize.

"Pierce and I used to go see local bands play at the pub after our football matches."

"Used to?"

Simon sips on his drink. "He doesn't like being away from the family. He's a sucker."

"A sucker?" I ask. "Or a man in love."

That gets me a smile. "Fine. A man in love. But I miss our nights out. Pierce is my closest mate. Can't fault the guy for falling in love, but sometimes I feel like everyone is passing me by."

I sigh. "I know the feeling."

"Yeah?"

Simon's fingers toy with the hem of my leggings.

"Ever since my divorce, the store has been my life. And I was fine with it. But now that my siblings are falling in love I feel stuck. I want so much more."

"Hopefully you'll get it all, love," Simon whispers in my ear.

Being with him makes me think I can get it. That I can have it all. Expand my shop, have him, and finally—*finally*—get the town off my back.

The band starts a new song. Even worse than the last.

"Do they know how bad they are?" It cuts the tension swirling around us.

"I didn't realize it'd be a showcase like this." Simon pulls a flyer out of his pocket. "It said the Flying Toaster Machine. I like them."

I scan the orange paper in his hand and find his mistake. "This is the Flying Toaster Machine Take Two. They are way different from the real band."

"Christ. I can't believe I subjected this to you on our first real date."

I shift, leaning against Simon's bent leg. "Aren't all good first dates memorable?"

"Want a way to make it more memorable?"

Simon's fingers slip under my T-shirt. Warmth seeps through me at the slight touch.

"What do you have in mind?" My voice is breathy.

"Once this godforsaken band is done, I want to take you back to your place and worship you. Show you everything I love about this sexy as fuck body that you have."

His fingers curl into my side as he takes my earlobe between his teeth. Heat gathers in my core.

"Yeah?"

"Get you all hot and bothered." Simon's voice gets growly. The scruff on his jaw against the soft skin of my cheek has my fingers sinking into his forearm. "Perhaps see what new lingerie you have on under this."

"What makes you think I have something new on under here?"

Simon sweeps my hair back. "I guess that's something I'll have to discover once I get you back into bed."

"Can we go back now?" His words have me wet. I'm ready to leave this band behind and get Simon inside of me.

"Oh no, love." Simon pulls his hand away from me and leans back. A rush of cool air moves in where he was. "We're going to enjoy the rest of the show and then we'll put on our own show."

"You're evil."

"It'll make it that much better when you come, love."

"Will it?"

"You don't believe me?"

I lean back, dropping a kiss onto the corner of his mouth. "Maybe I'll do the same to you."

"That's just mean, love."

"Little taste of your own medicine."

"Fuck. This is going to be a long night."

One that I can't wait to continue when we get back to my place.

Chapter Nineteen

SIMON

Finally.

Fucking *finally*.

I don't think I've ever heard a band play for so long. After teasing Layla, all I wanted to do was bring her back to her apartment and have my way with her.

But no.

I wanted to tease her. To ramp up her need to make it even more explosive tonight. Every minute I spend with her is like foreplay. And it's going to make when I finally get between her legs even better.

As soon as the last note is played, Layla's on her feet.

"Move it, slowpoke."

Her arse is across the street before I can throw away the empty cans.

"Let's go, Belvy."

Layla looks like an angel standing under the soft light of her porch. Checking the streets, I jog across to the woman I can't stop thinking about. She's backing her way inside. As soon as I'm in, I kick the door shut behind me and I'm on her.

"You are evil."

Both of us are fighting for control. This kiss is messy and hot. She nips at my lip, tugging it between her teeth.

"Can you blame me? How do you manage to make a fucking T-shirt so sexy?" I pull at the knot, letting it unravel in my hands.

Layla pushes me off her and whips her top over her head.

"Is this what you were working on the other day?"

"Maybe." Layla drags a single finger over the cup of a forest-green bra. It has two tiny bows embroidered on each cup, drawing my attention to her nipples. Her very hard nipples.

"I can't believe you made this." I step closer, dropping a kiss just above one bow.

"I made it just for you."

"You did?" I drag one strap down her shoulder. "Is this all you made?"

Layla shakes her head.

"Are you going to show me more?"

Stepping closer, Layla walks her pink-painted tipped fingers up my chest. "I shouldn't. Give you a taste of your own medicine."

"Now who's mean?" I rub a hand over my fabric-clad dick.

Layla steps up onto the bottom step, now at eye-level with me. "Go upstairs and wait on my bed."

"Oh yeah? And if I don't?" I quirk a brow at her.

"Then I guess you won't get to find out if the bottoms match."

That gets me up the stairs faster than I can remember running. Layla's chuckles follow me up. "You better hurry, love."

Luna is snoozing on the couch. I leave her be, doing

exactly as Layla wants. Grabbing the back of my shirt, I tug it off and toe out of my shoes.

I lie back against the headboard and wait. Each second feels like an eternity. I want this woman with a fierce longing I've never felt. I want to spend all of my nights with her. All my days.

I'm addicted, and it's only been a few weeks.

The soft sound of feet breaks my thoughts. Layla is standing there in her bra and underwear. A matching set.

"Christ, Layla." I rub my hand over my dick, trying to will him down.

"Uh-uh. No touching." She strolls over to the bed. A damp spot darkens the green fabric of her panties. "That's my job."

"You want to move faster then?"

"Patience, Simon," Layla whispers in my ear.

"I don't have much."

Layla's tongue licks a path down my jaw. "You'll have some, don't worry."

Her hand settles on my chest, an icy chill spreading through me.

"Fuck! What is that?"

"What do you think?"

Layla's hand trails down my chest, the ice melting down my chest. Her hand is slow, teasing. The cool gives way to heat, making my dick harder.

My hands fist in the sheets as she dips it lower under my boxers.

"I like seeing you squirm. A little taste of what you did to me earlier."

Layla licks the water off my chest, flicking her tongue over my abs. I want to run my hands all over her. Kiss every inch of her body to make up for the teasing. I want her. Every piece of her she'll give me.

"Should I put you out of your misery?"

Layla's mouth closes over the fabric covering my dick.

"Yes, yes you should."

Her smile is sinful. "I guess I should."

Pulling my pants and boxers down, my dick springs free, slapping me in the stomach. Hungry eyes are studying it, like she can't wait to have a taste.

"Are you going to—"

Layla cuts me off with a long lick of the vein of the underside of my dick.

"Fuck yes!"

Warm lips wrap around the head, swirling around. All I want to do is sink my hands into her hair and guide her movements. Take exactly what she's giving me.

"Mmm," she hums around my dick. She pulls off and says, "I love how good you feel in my mouth." The look she gives me is downright sinful.

Her lips close around me, working me over.

Fuck. I can't take it anymore. Threading my hands into her silky hair, I guide her movements. Her eyes are on locked on mine. Every bob has me that closer to releasing down her throat.

Except I don't want to. I want to be deep inside her when that happens.

"I need to be inside you."

Layla pulls off me with a pop, wiping her mouth with her hand. Reaching to the side table, she grabs a condom and tosses it at me.

I waste no time rolling it down my hard length. Layla shimmies off her underwear, throwing them at me. I take a whiff, smelling how hot she is for me.

"Have you been like this all night?"

"You know I have." She settles over me, taking my dick in hand. "I should make you wait, but I can't."

"You feel amazing." Each slow inch she sinks down drives me crazy.

"So do you. So good. So big." Her words are stuttered as she rolls her hips.

Grabbing her hips, I start to move her. We're in sync. Layla is a goddess above me as she takes her own pleasure. My touch on her is bruising, squeezing her each time she comes down.

I find her clit, rubbing circles over it. I'm ready to feel her come undone.

"Oh, Simon."

"Come for me, Layla."

I sit up, taking her in a kiss. I can't resist.

Our tongues tangle as I get closer to release. The same as Layla, based on the way she's strangling my dick to within an inch of its life.

"Yes, yes, yes!" Her shouts echo around the room as she comes. "Oh God, yes!"

"Fuck." Flipping us over, I pound into her. The way she's coming around me, it doesn't take more than a few thrusts before I'm erupting like a volcano.

"Layla!"

Holy shit. I wouldn't be surprised if I black out, I come so hard. Her pulsing around me extends my orgasm.

Damn. Does it ever feel incredible.

My body goes limp as I collapse on top of her. Layla wraps me in her arms, keeping me close. Our breaths are heavy, filling the room.

Neither of us moves as our breathing evens out.

"Simon. That was…"

"I know." I press a kiss into her sweat-slicked skin. Her fingers drag through my hair. I could stay like this and never get tired.

It felt better than anything I've ever experienced. Based on Layla's reaction, it's the same for her.

I never thought it would feel this good with her. Even this small part of her that she's giving me won't be enough.

"You know, maybe we should have a real first date again."

I smile against her chest. "As long as we get to do that? I'll give you all the dates you could ever want."

Chapter Twenty

LAYLA

"You ready?"

Simon pulls the shirt down over this head, covering those delicious abs of his.

"I am if you are." The smirk on his face tells me he caught me staring.

"Yes." I shake the dirty thoughts from my head. Simon looks good in my apartment like this. He looks at home here. He slid into my life like he's always been a part of it.

It's a feeling I didn't realize I missed. Or if I even had it to begin with.

"Your words say yes, but that look on your face says you want to go back to bed." Simon wraps his arms around me, dropping his forehead to mine. "I'd be onboard with bed."

"Of course you would." I push him off me, but he doesn't budge. "But I have a fun surprise for you."

"If it's more of that lingerie…"

My smile is downright evil as I steal a quick kiss from him. I love how much he loves the lingerie I design. Even more how much he wants to tear it off me. Ever so gently, of course.

"Maybe if you come with me, I'll show you what I've got on underneath here."

Simon lets out a deep groan. "Now how am I supposed to concentrate with that thought in my head all day, love? That's just cruel."

"Then let's get going."

This time, I duck out of his hold and head to the door. It's the perfect summer day in Dixon. The Tetons look as majestic as ever in the distance. Blake and Gemma wanted a few days to themselves before the wedding this weekend, so it was the perfect time to surprise Simon.

"Where are we going?" Wrapping an arm around me, Simon pulls me close. I find the back pocket of his jeans, slipping my hand inside and giving his ass a good squeeze.

We fall into an easy pace, the sidewalk busy with summer tourists.

"You're like Willow. Always asking questions and can never take a surprise."

"I don't like surprises. Surprises in my line of work usually mean a bad thing."

"Well, this isn't work. And this isn't a bad thing. Relax."

"I'd relax a lot more if we were still at your place," he whispers into my hair before dropping a kiss on my head.

Butterflies erupt in my stomach. I thought this thing with Simon would be a lot harder. I've never liked showing affection in public, but maybe that was because of Brad. He never would have wanted to anyway.

With Simon, everything is easy. Holding his hand. Kissing him. Laughing with him.

Turns out pretending the hot Brit is your fiancé isn't all that difficult.

"Later. Now, here we are."

"How does it take no time at all to get anywhere in this town?" Simon mutters as I pull the door open.

"Because everything is on the main drag."

One of the perks of living in a small town.

"Where are we?" Simon is looking around.

"You took me on a real date, so I figured I could take you out."

The Train Museum is in one of the small buildings on the street. If you didn't know about it, it's likely that you would pass right by it and never realize it's there. With only a small sign, it's completely unassuming. It's not frequently visited. It's one of the many reasons I knew I could bring Simon here without a lot of gawking eyes.

"A train museum?" There's awe in his voice as his gaze comes back to mine.

"Do you like it?"

Simon closes the distance between us as his mouth crashes down on mine. His fingers tangle in my hair as he swipes his tongue along my lips, demanding entrance.

The moment his tongue touches mine, the dam on the emotions I've kept locked up bursts.

I can't keep my hands off him as we both get swept up in this kiss. It's not just me getting lost in the sensations. I can feel everything Simon is pouring into this kiss as well.

It has my toes curling and goosebumps erupting everywhere.

I never want this feeling to end. If I could bottle it up and keep it with me every day, I would.

Except someone's throat clearing brings us back to reality.

"Do you two have tickets?"

Simon's pupils are dilated as he stares down at me.

"We do," I tell whoever is behind the counter.

"Oh, Layla. I should've known that was you."

"Mrs. Lewis." Of course she's the one working here today. "Lovely to see you."

Her thin lips disappear from her face as she looks at me with contempt.

"Here's a map. Please make sure you don't touch any of the exhibits."

The smile on my face is as syrupy sweet as you can get. Completely fake. "That won't be a problem. Have a nice day."

"Mm-hmm." She goes back to the papers sitting on her desk.

"Why is she giving me the evil eye? I've never done anything to her."

"It's because you're engaged to me," I whisper to Simon as we head inside.

Simon peers behind him, turning back to me. "Christ, she's giving me the look. Would it be bad if I mooned her?"

"Oh my God, don't you dare!"

"Might be the highlight of her life."

Linking my hand with his, I tug him past the information booth and into the first room.

"Don't make me march you right back out of here."

Simon places his hand over his heart. "I promise I'll be on my best behavior. Hell, I have half a mind to touch everything in here if I didn't think she'd call the bobbies on us."

I snicker. "The bobbies? You're so British."

"You love it." He pulls me into his side, nibbling on my neck.

"Stop!" I try to shove him off. "I'm serious. You'll get us kicked out."

"Well, we can't have that, now can we?" Simon straightens. "Best behavior. Promise."

Simon's voice is playful as he looks around us. Model trains are set up around the room, with placards providing detailed information. Vintage train travel posters, yellowing at the corners, line the walls. Large Edison bulbs hang over head, giving it an old-timey vibe. The last time I was here was probably in fifth grade for a field trip.

"It's not too nerdy?"

Simon huffs out a laugh, scrubbing a hand over his face. A shy look comes over his face. I don't think I've ever seen him look like this before. Bashful almost.

"Then that would make me a nerd, love."

"You? With all these muscles?" I poke his bicep. "Please."

"I wasn't always like this." Simon meanders through the small room, taking everything in. "I was a scrawny thing in primary school. Got picked on a lot."

It tugs at my heartstrings, thinking of Simon getting made fun of at school. It's hard to imagine given his current job and his protective nature, not to mention his amazing physique.

"I was never the cool kid. I always kept to myself."

"How'd you meet Pierce and Charlotte?"

This draws a laugh out of him as we move into the next room, which is dominated with parts from actual trains rather than models.

"Pierce and I started playing football together and haven't stopped."

"I don't know how you're friends with the way you two play together."

"If you want to call it 'playing.' Lousy cheat is what he is."

"So you play football together?" I steer him back to the topic at hand.

"Ay. After a few nights out at the pub, we became friends. He's an easy guy to like."

I walk around one of the engines in the middle of the room. "And now here you are playing bodyguard in America."

"And following all the pretty girls around."

"What a sweet talker." Except his words have butterflies exploding low in my belly.

Simon's eyes are all over the place, exploring the grand room we're in, but mine are only on him.

I don't know how I got lucky enough to stumble upon this man. For the last few years, I was adamant that I didn't need anyone. Relying on someone made me vulnerable, and I never wanted to feel like that again.

Not after my divorce.

I was fine being on my own. Running Pinstripes & Push-Ups exactly how I wanted without any outside interference.

It should scare me, how easily I can rely on Simon. He's here without being overbearing or controlling. Quietly supporting me in anything I do.

God, how did I get so lucky to find someone like him when I wasn't even looking?

It should have me locking up my heart, keeping it hidden away where it can remain safely unbroken. Simon is temporary. Only here for the duration of the wedding and then he'll be jetting back off to London.

Except seeing the way he's smiling at the train he's inspecting has my body automatically reaching out to him.

Neither of us are ready to let this man go.

Shaking myself from the thoughts of Simon leaving, I stand on the other side of the model from him.

"Enjoying yourself?"

His smile is big and bright. "It's one of the first diesel engines used in America. It's brilliant."

Big green eyes are filled with the wonder and excitement of a little kid.

"I'm glad."

The sound of a train from the next room have Simon grabbing my hand and pulling me through the museum.

The chugging of the locomotive on the wall across from us is the only sound in the room as videos of different trains play on a loop. Simon pulls me down on the bench next to him. It's a zen-like experience.

"Tell me why you like trains so much."

His fingertips trace the lines on my palm.

"It was something I did with my granddad. He did it with his granddad before, and it was something that only the two of us did together."

"He sounds like a good guy." My eyes stay fixed on where our hands are joined.

"He was. Whenever my mum's boyfriend dumped her, she'd be a wreck, so I'd go stay with them for a few weeks. He'd take me to see the trains, almost as a way to distract me from the shit going on in my life."

"This is why you started a security firm." I rest my chin on his shoulder, running my hand through his hair. "You're a protector."

"I wouldn't say that."

Clasping his face in my hands, I turn so he's focused solely on me. "Of course you are. That's what brought you here. What started your company. Why you stepped in to help me. You protect the people you care about."

"I do." His deep-green eyes are glued to mine. "I hated how they treated Mum. Half of the time, they ignored me. Treated me like I didn't exist. I hated it. She always thought she had to have a man to feel special. By the time the last bloke dumped her when I was starting year ten, she got fed up. That's when we moved in with my grandparents."

I can't imagine anyone ignoring Simon. This sweet little boy only looking for affection, and his mom looking for it in all the wrong places. It has my heart reaching out for his. I hated that he had to go through this at all.

"Does your mom still live with them?"

"My granddad died a few years ago. She lives nearby with her new husband so Grandmum isn't alone."

"Do you like this new guy?" My fingers idly play with his hair. I want to know everything about this man.

He nods. "I do. He's a good guy. Nothing like the pieces of shit she used to date."

"You know, you're nothing like I thought you'd be."

Simon shifts, pulling my legs over his lap. We're impossibly close, yet not close enough for my liking. "Oh yeah?"

Those strong hands of his run up and down my leg. Because it's the perfect summer day, we're the only people in here.

"You showed up with all these muscles with those dark sunglasses, dressed in all black looking like you were trying to be a super agent. I thought you'd stand on the sidelines and keep an eye on everyone from there."

"I'd hardly call myself a super agent," he scoffs. Of course that's what he picks up on.

I ignore him. "But then you stepped in for me when you hardly knew me."

"I'd step in again, love." Simon smiles down at me, his hand sliding farther up my leg.

"I'm really glad you did. Not that we have to go through with this whole charade, because God forbid a woman sell lingerie, but still. I'm glad you're here and that I've gotten to know you."

"I'm finding I quite like you now that I know you, Layla."

Layla.

I don't know if I'll ever get used to hearing him say my name. The way it rolls off his tongue in that accent. I could bottle it up and listen to it forever.

"And I love learning all these new bits about you. No matter if you think they're nerdy."

Simon puffs out his chest. "I make Trainspotting cool."

"Whatever you say, my little nerd."

"You mean badass."

"As long as you're here, I'll call you whatever you want."

"I really could get used to this."

"What? Nature?"

A laugh burbles out of me. This woman never ceases to put a smile on my face. "I meant being out here with you."

Layla turns on her heel, the creek burbling into the lake as we walk along the property. "I like getting to show you this place."

Everything about it is beautiful. The moon hangs high in the sky, glittering off the lake we stop beside. The mountains are bright, even at night, from the snow sitting on their peaks. Even in the middle of summer.

"What's your favorite part about living here?" My fingers play with hers, stepping farther into her space.

"The air."

"That's your favorite part?" I quirk a brow up at her.

She nods, giving me a look like I'm an idiot. "It's the clean mountain air. Nothing like you get in the city."

"So London wouldn't do it for you then?"

"Sorry, Dixon is it for me."

It's another reminder of how our time together is

coming to an end. That in a week, I'll be heading back home to London and she'll stay here in Dixon.

A place she loves. A place that is thousands of miles away from the city. A place that could never give her what she loves about Dixon.

Two complete opposites who are only together for a short while.

"What's your favorite thing about London?"

Layla's question brings me back to present.

"The people."

"Really?"

"Yeah. You meet so many different people in the city, you never get bored."

Layla steps closer to me, walking her fingers up my chest. "Are you talking about women?"

"Fuck no," I answer immediately.

"Smart man."

Layla moves to continue walking again, but I grab her around the waist and pull her into me.

"There's never enough time for that. Work takes up my entire day." I tip her chin up so her eyes meet mine. "Maybe if there was a certain blonde bombshell in London, I might take notice, but not other women."

Pushing up onto her tiptoes, she lays a big kiss on me. It's needy and urgent, her tongue demanding access.

Fuck. Why are kisses with Layla so damn good? I could spend the entire day kissing her and not be bothered by a single thing.

Before her, my entire life revolved around work. It wasn't a lie to protect her feelings. No woman has ever caught my attention.

Layla? A few weeks with her and she's working her way into every part of me. This spunky, confident spitfire is everything I've always wanted in a woman.

Fuck. I don't know what I'm going to do when I go back to London without her.

"You want to know why this is one of my favorite spots?" Layla breaks the kiss and steps back.

"Why's that?" I growl. I want to spend less time talking and more time savoring this woman.

"It's nice and quiet for doing naughty things."

That grabs my attention. "What kind of naughty things?"

I'm hoping for the kind that will make my growing dick happy.

Grabbing the hem of her dress, she pulls it up and over her head, revealing another gorgeous set of lingerie. This set is black, laced with gold flowers. The mesh fabric leaves little to the imagination.

Something I also love. This woman designs and wears her own lingerie.

Fucking sexy as hell.

I'm not paying attention when her bra and panties hit me square in the face. The moon shines bright off all the exposed skin of hers.

Very naked skin as she jumps into the lake.

"Skinny-dipping?"

She stands, the water hitting just below her tits. Fuck, they look delicious from here.

"You going to join me?"

Toeing out of my shoes, I strip out of my clothes and jump into the water.

"Holy fuck!" It's like thousands of tiny icicles are pricking my skin. "Warn a man next time!"

"Do you need me to warm you up?" Layla swims over to me. The water barely comes up to my chest. The night air does little to help keep me warm.

"I'm pretty sure my dick has shriveled up and fallen off.

Fuck, it's freezing."

"Do you need me to check?" Layla wraps herself around me like a koala bear.

"I mean, maybe."

Not that I'd ever turn down having her hands on me.

Small hands drift down my chest. Her fingers wrap around my soft length. The slightest touch from her has him perking up.

"Looks like he's still functioning."

I nip at her bottom lip. "I'm glad I have you here to test him out."

"And now you know why this is my favorite place."

I press kisses down her jaw. Tug her earlobe between my teeth. "Mmm, yes. I do like getting to do all the naughty things with you."

The cold is long forgotten as Layla and I explore one another. Water laps against our skin—now feeling good against the heat swirling around us.

"I could stay out here all night."

Layla leans back, floating on the water.

Fuck me, does she ever look gorgeous like this, swaying gently in the moonlight looking like a goddess.

"Even if we turn into a couple of prunes?"

Layla sits up, hair slick against her. "Even then."

Lights shine over the top of the lake, tires crackling over dirt.

"Fuck. What is that?"

"Shit. Someone's there! Get out!" Layla pushes me toward the side of the lake. Rushing out, I grab her hand and hoist her out.

"Here. Put this on." I chuck my shirt at her as I'm pulling my pants on, just as the car comes to a stop in front of us. Finding my undershirt, I pull it down fast.

Maybe we won't look like we were just buck-ass naked in the water.

"Let me do the talking," Layla says on a shiver.

Now that we're not wrapped up in one another, the cool night air settles around us.

The door opens and a large man with a wide-brimmed cowboy hat steps out.

Fucking hell. We better not get arrested.

"Evenin' folks."

"Hey Sheriff Hamilton." Layla holds up a hand, shielding her from the lights of his flashlight.

"Layla Winchester? Is that you?"

"It's me."

"Heard the noise over here and wanted to make sure it wasn't troublemakers. Didn't know it was you."

"Troublemakers?" I whisper to her.

She smacks my chest.

"Why were you out here this time of night, Sheriff?"

The sheriff shakes his head, dropping the flashlight. "Extra security."

"Isn't that my job?" I ask, this time not bothering to hide my voice. It's the whole reason I'm here in the first place.

"With the wedding going on and all these fancy Brits here, we want to make sure the property is secure against any trespassers." He ignores me.

"I appreciate it, Sheriff. But we're all good over here." It's the whole reason I'm here.

He tips his hat at Layla. "I reckon you are. You two take care of yourselves, now."

"Thanks, Sheriff. Tell the family I said hi."

He waves before getting into the car and heading back out to the dirt road leading around the property.

"Shit. That was close." I blow out a breath I didn't realize I was holding.

Layla bursts out laughing. "You should see your face!"

"Me? What if we were arrested?"

My white shirt clings to Layla, showing off all her curves.

"You couldn't sweet-talk an old man into not arresting us?" Layla wraps her arms around my neck.

"I don't think he would've listened to me." I hoist Layla up, her legs going around my waist. "You on the other hand? You could talk your way out of anything."

Layla drags her finger down my jaw. "Maybe I could talk you *into* coming home with me tonight?"

"You don't have to ask me twice."

Chapter Twenty-Two

LAYLA

"**I** can't believe the police found us."

I unlock my front door and push it open, Simon hot on my heels.

"When I said I didn't want to be arrested for indecent exposure, that wasn't a challenge."

"It's not like they would have arrested us."

Simon gives me a devious smile. "Look at you. Corrupting poor, sweet, little old me."

"I don't think anything about you is sweet."

He quirks a brow in my direction. "Definitely not after what we did last night."

"You're incorrigible."

Heading to the bathroom to get towels to clean up, I flip on the light and gasp at my reflection. Makeup is caked under my eyes, and I look like I have two black eyes. It's smudged in other places.

It looks like I went ten rounds with a boxer.

Have I looked like this the entire way home?

And why didn't Simon tell me?

"Everything okay?" Simon calls from the living room.

"Uhh, give me a second."

Digging around in the drawers, I try to find a wash-cloth to clean up my face.

"What's going on?" Simon's eyes lock with mine in the mirror.

"Why didn't you tell me I look like the daughter of Frankenstein?" I wave my hand around my face.

"It wouldn't have been polite." It comes out almost sounding like a question.

Blowing out a frustrated breath, I find a cloth and turn on the water. Simon's hand on my wrist stops me.

"Let me."

"I can do it."

His breath is hot on my neck. "Allow me, love."

Hopping up on the counter, I watch as his deep-green eyes scan over my face. There's a question written there, but his soft hands swipe over my cheek. My eyes close as his touch tenderly moves over my face.

"Why do you wear all this?"

His question hits me square in the chest. I'm thankful my eyes are closed because I've never talked about it with anyone.

"I just like to wear makeup. No real reason."

"See, you saying no real reason tells me there's a reason."

I peek one eye open at him. "Is this what makes you so good at your job?"

The corner of his mouth pulls up into a smile. "Yes. Now, tell me the truth."

"And if I don't?"

Simon crosses his arms, his damp T-shirt clinging to his biceps. His eyes are locked on mine in a game of chicken. I break first.

"I started doing it after my divorce."

Simon runs the cloth under the warm water and goes back to wiping off the running makeup. He doesn't say anything. My eyes close, not wanting to look at him as I rip off old Band-Aids on wounds that have long since healed.

"I lost a part of myself. We were married for about four years when he decided he wanted to run for mayor. Every event we went to, I had to be perfect. Tan suit, sensible shoes. Even the length of my hair was a point of contention. I couldn't put a toe out of line if he wanted to be elected. By the time I realized how much I'd changed, I barely recognized myself. I hated how much I'd changed. At that point, Brad and I were strangers. We were going through the motions. I felt like the town pariah because I left Brad. I didn't want to be stuck in a loveless marriage. So I left. This town is so full of gossips, that I didn't want to give anyone a reason to talk about me. So I started watching makeup tutorials."

"Like your armor against the world."

Opening my eyes, Simon is close.

"Exactly. It made me feel beautiful. Daring and dramatic looks. If anyone was going to be talking about me, they couldn't comment on how I looked." My voice shakes as I say the words. "Yet, it seems like no matter what I do, I'm not good enough for this town."

I never wanted to be the topic of discussion after my divorce, even though I knew it would be. News like that runs rampant in small towns. Dixon is no exception.

"Layla."

"Don't tell me I'm being ridiculous."

"You don't need all of this."

"You don't have to say that." I push him away, but he doesn't budge.

Damn Simon and all his muscles.

"I'm serious." Simon drops his hands to the counter on

either side of my hips. His eyes are piercing straight through me. "You are the most beautiful woman I've ever met. You don't need all this."

Simon presses his lips to my forehead. To my nose. To each temple. Each cheek. A rush of emotions washes over me at his tender touch.

"Fucking gorgeous, Layla. With or without all this, you are the most beautiful, most generous person I have ever met. You are passionate. And driven. And so fucking strong. I don't know how you deal with being in this town when they treat you like this. You have the biggest heart and they should be lucky to have you. I know I'm lucky to be on your arm. Luckiest fucking bastard in the world."

My breath catches in my throat as I fist my hands in his shirt, keeping him close. The rapid beat of my heat is threatening to burst out of my chest.

Never once did Brad say anything like this to me when we were married. Sure, he occasionally told me that I looked nice. But never this.

Never a declaration of how beautiful I am. I've known this man for all of three weeks and he's unlocked a piece of me that I didn't know was still there.

"Simon, I…"

I don't even know what to say.

"Don't say anything. Let me show you how much I adore you." Simon sweeps me into his arms, carrying me into my room and setting me on the edge of my bed.

Deft fingers unfasten the buttons of the shirt I'm wearing. Warm lips press kisses into my skin as Simon pulls the shirt off my body. Cool air hits my nipples, pulling them tight.

"So fucking gorgeous," he whispers before taking one hard bud between his teeth.

"Gah!" I arch into his touch as his hands roam up and

down my sides. The slightest caress of his against my skin sets me on fire. It's like he knows exactly how to make my body light up with need. Want. A hunger I've never felt before.

Simon releases my nipple with a pop before kissing his way over to give the other the same attention. The scratchiness from his jaw has my core aching.

"More."

"More what, love?" Simon presses another kiss in the valley between my breasts.

"Of that. All of it."

"Patience." Simon tips me back on the bed, his eyes dark with lust. "It'll be worth it. I promise."

Simon stands, grabbing the back of his shirt and pulling it over his head, exposing the hard planes of his chest.

I want to run my fingers over every muscle. Feel them flex under my touch.

Simon's hands grab my pants and pull them down my legs, tossing them behind him. In nothing but a scrap of underwear, his hands walk up my legs.

His touch does nothing to cool the fiery need that is now raging through me. I want to feel this man everywhere. To have him brand himself on me in a way I've never had before. To own and possess me.

Dragging his tongue over the lace of my thong, he bites the hem.

"You better not ruin these."

I feel his smile against my hipbone.

"I think you're doing that all on your own." He hooks a finger around them and rubs it down my pussy, brushing ever so slightly against my clit. "Someone is needy."

"For you? Yes."

Simon takes his time sliding the underwear down my

legs. He never takes his eyes off me. The connection is palpable as he makes his way back up my naked body.

"Is this where you need me?" Simon flicks his tongue over my pulsing clit. "Or is it here?" He slips his tongue between my folds.

"Yes."

"To which?"

I hear the laugh in his voice.

"Both. I want—"

He cuts me off as his lips close around my clit and he sinks a thick digit inside me.

"Yes!"

The way he curls his finger inside of me has heat racing down my spine. My core throbs as he assaults my clit, licking and sucking. Driving me wild with need.

Pushing my legs farther apart, Simon delves his tongue even deeper inside of me, hitting a spot only he seems to be able to find.

"Gorgeous. Gorgeous, love. I'm so lucky I get you like this."

"I'm so close." I find purchase in his hair, grabbing hold of the short strands. He doesn't stop. His tongue and fingers work me over, twisting and turning, to push me right over the edge as my orgasm flashes through me.

It's like my entire body is made of electricity, zinging and pulsing as Simon strokes me through an intense orgasm. My entire body goes lax as he sits back on his feet.

"I rather enjoy adoring you." Simon drops a kiss on my stomach before standing, wiping a hand over his mouth. It's the hottest thing—seeing my release coating his lips.

Shucking off his pants, Simon grabs a condom and rolls it down his leaking cock. If I thought I was needy before, it's nothing compared to now.

Even the one orgasm isn't enough to quell the need I

feel for this man. Seeing how hard I make Simon gets me ready for round two.

Taking me in his arms, he lies back against the headboard. His lips find mine in a lazy kiss. Hands roaming, our tongues tangle as I taste the evidence of how good this man makes me feel.

I drink him in, needing every bit of him that I can get. His cock is rock-hard between my thighs.

"You ready for round two, love?" Simon pulls back, brushing my hair off my face.

Reaching down, I take his dick in hand and line myself up. I sink down, slow inch by slow inch until he fills me up, stretching me in the best possible way.

"Fuck. You feel incredible," Simon hisses. He rotates his hips. "So fucking good."

Wrapping his arms around me, I set a lazy pace. My movements are small, and I revel in how good he feels inside me.

His hands grasp my ass, moving me over him.

Our breaths mix as our shared desire builds.

It's like a living thing inside me. I can't get enough of this man.

"You going to come for me again?" His accent is thicker. The need in his voice is apparent. His thumb strums my clit.

My movements become more frenzied the closer I get to my second release of the night.

"So close." I nibble on his lip. My fingers dig into his pecs, trying to hold on as this man takes me over the cliff once again.

"Simon! Oh God, Simon."

A few more hard pumps and Simon is coming right along with me.

"Fuck." His neck is strained as the vein there throbs.

I cling to Simon as he holds me through my release. My entire body is spent in the best possible way. There's no way I'll ever get enough of this man in the short time we have left.

Slipping out, Simon lays me on the bed before heading to the bathroom. My eyes stay glued on the tight globes of his ass, drinking him in.

His smile is playful as he comes back. The moonlight dances across his skin as he leans over me, cleaning me up. The gentleness of his touch has my heart banging around in my chest.

What have I done to deserve this man?

Settling in next to me, Simon pulls the duvet over us. I snuggle into his side, his arms wrapping around me, happily sated from another orgasm.

"Thank you," I whisper into his chest.

Strong fingers rake through my hair. "You never need to thank me, love."

Sleep starts to tug at my consciousness. Lying here in Simon's arms, I feel safe. Cared for. Loved, even. It's like everything I've been missing has been dropped into my arms.

"I'd adore you every fucking day if I could." Simon's whispered words are the last thing I hear before sleep takes me.

If only.

Chapter Twenty-Three

SIMON

"Thanks for coming with me, mate." Pierce claps me on the shoulder as I open the door to the bar where Blake's stag party is being held.

It's still early, so it's not as crowded as it could be. Christmas lights hang from the ceiling. Country music is playing loudly over the speakers. Seats made from old saddles line the front of the wooden bar.

It's everything you'd expect a place like this to be.

"You were worried about security?" I eye him. Walking up to the bar, I order us two pints.

Not that it would matter. I sent a few guys here earlier just to make sure. We don't make our presence known, so no one would be alerted to Piece being here. It makes my job easier.

Without any threats or rabid paparazzi, I can breathe a little better at night.

Pierce scoffs next to me. "Here? No. I used that as an excuse so you wouldn't sit in your room all night."

"Why would you assume I'd sit in my room all night?"

"Because Layla is out with the girls tonight."

"So you assumed I'd just stay in?"

I sip on the beer that's set in front of me and pass over a twenty.

"Mate,"—Pierce claps me on the shoulder—"the only time I've seen you lately is with Layla. You know, your fiancée."

I don't like the way he says that. *Your fiancée.*

Almost like he needs to remind me of who Layla is to me. Not that I could forget. She's all I've been thinking about lately.

I want to soak up every ounce of time with her I can get. Because next week, I'll be back in London.

Alone.

I hate the pang that hits every time I think about it.

"Sorry if I enjoy spending time with her."

"You're getting married"—there's that tone again—"it's not like you're not going to be seeing her again soon. Right?" He quirks a brow in my direction.

Except I won't be. Not unless I bump into her if she's visiting her family in London. Once this wedding is over, there goes my fake fiancée.

A sinking weight drops in my stomach. I don't know if I'm ready to deal with that—not seeing Layla every day.

The way her smile lights up her entire face.

The way her eyes always seem to find mine in a crowd.

Her fierce drive.

I'm not ready to face life without Layla yet.

"Simon! Pierce! Over here," Mason calls from across the bar.

His words pull me out of my spiraling thoughts. I glance at Pierce and see that his eyes still on me in a studious way.

"What's with you tonight?" I ask, trying to deflect this attention from him.

"Nothing. Just glad that you decided to come out with me tonight. I miss my mate."

"You'll have me all to yourself once we get back to London."

He laughs as we make our way through the crowd. Blake and a group of guys, some of whom I recognize, are gathered around a group of tables on one side of the bar.

"Simon. Glad you could join us." Blake holds out a hand to me.

"Thanks, mate."

"Who would want to miss celebrating you tonight?" Pierce wraps an arm around his shoulder. This man is comfortable no matter where he goes.

Blake holds his glass up in cheers. "Thanks guys for being here. And hey, soon enough we'll be celebrating Simon."

"Made any plans for that?" Pierce elbows me in the side.

"Plans for what?" I sip on my beer.

"Plans for what, he asks?" Pierce laughs. "Have you and Layla set a date yet?"

I shrug a shoulder, trying to stay casual. "We haven't talked about it."

"Really?" Blake chimes in. "Gemma had a date within a week."

"Isn't your schedule insane though?" I ask him. "You're directing a TV show."

"Writing," he corrects, "and it does make for a crazy schedule. We didn't want to wait."

"So why are you waiting? Don't you want to marry my sister?" Mason gives me a look that might tear down a lesser man.

If he knew the truth, he'd probably kill me.

"Like I said,"—I gulp down the rest of my beer—"we

didn't want to take away from Blake and Gemma's big day, so we decided to wait."

"Will you get married here or in London?" Blake asks.

"I need a refill. Can I get anyone anything else?"

I don't wait for anyone to respond, cutting through the growing crowd to make it to the bar.

"What's with you tonight?"

Of course Pierce followed me over to the bar.

"Why all the third degree? Is it really necessary?" I flag down the bartender to order another beer.

"Maybe if you weren't being so dodgy."

"Can you just let it be?" I'm ready to snap.

"Alright, chill out. Not sure why questions about your fiancée are getting you so riled up. It's not like you, mate."

It's the final straw. "Because it's not real!" I snap at him.

Pierce's eyes go wide at my outburst. "Are you fucking kidding me?"

Shit. Shit, shit, shit. Of all the things to make me break, that did it.

"Outside. Now."

Ignoring the drink set in front of me, I push Pierce ahead of me, moving through the crowded bar.

"What do you mean it's fake?" Pierce whispers at me. Downtown Dixon is the place to be tonight. Crowds are gathered out on the main drag. Patrons spill out of the bars onto patios, pints of beer in hand.

I scrub a hand down my face. "She needed help and I was there."

"You know this isn't in your job description, right? We only needed you to make sure paparazzi didn't track us down and ruin the wedding."

"I know, you wanker."

"Then how the hell did you get yourself into this?"

I don't think I've ever seen Pierce like this. He's one of the most easygoing people I know. Nothing bothers him. Unless it's with his family.

And Layla is family.

"Brad was giving her grief about her business. Everyone in town has been all over her about it and how it's not appropriate for a single woman to sell lingerie."

"And this culminated in you being her fiancé?"

"It was supposed to be a fake dating thing. Just during the wedding to get the town off her back while she tries to secure a new storefront. But then she was talking to these older women and it just slipped out."

"That you're getting married."

"Yes."

He stares at me. "Are you fucking kidding me?"

"I couldn't back down at that point. They would've eaten her alive, mate."

"Don't get me wrong, I love it here. But yeah, I guess sometimes the people here can be a little old-fashioned."

"A little? You should've seen the way these women were judging her. You'd think she was worshipping the devil the way they act."

Pierce leans against the side of the building, giving me an assessing stare. It's uncomfortable. "And you two were okay lying to everyone?"

"Fuck no." I shake my head. "Trust me, neither of us liked doing that. But if it helped Layla save her store? I'd do it again."

"As far as fake couples go, you're a pretty good one."

"Uh-huh."

Pierce groans. "Please tell me you're not sleeping with her."

I don't say a word. What can I say when he's already pissed?

"For fuck's sake, Simon! Which head are you thinking with?"

"You and Charlotte keep talking about wanting me to start dating."

"And this is how you took that? To be 'fake engaged' to my cousin? Christ, you really aren't thinking."

I wasn't. But I meant what I told him. I'd do it again to help Layla. I'd do anything she needed to help her. Because even though it's only been a few weeks, I'd lay down my life for her.

Christ. I'm so fucking in love with this woman, it's not even funny. What have I gotten myself into?

"What's going to happen when we leave next week? Did you think about that?"

"Maybe she'd want to come back to London with me…" It's a hopeful thought.

"Her life is here." Pierce is *oh so helpful* in pointing that out.

"I know, but it's worth a shot, right?"

"And the store you're helping her try and save?"

Fuck. I scrub a hand down my face.

"Look, I don't know what I'm going to do, but you can't tell anyone. Especially your wife."

A shoulder bumps into me from a passerby. I'm ready to call them out until I see who it is.

Fucking Brad.

"Gentlemen. I hope you're enjoying your evening out." He dips his head our way as he continues down the street.

The look on his face tells me nothing.

"Oh fuck. Do you think he heard us?" Pierce whispers.

"This is all your fault," I grumble.

"Mine? How is this my fault?"

"If you didn't keep poking and asking questions, I wouldn't have snapped."

He throws his hands up in defence. "I can't help it if I thought you were lying to me. Which, you were, mate."

He's not wrong. I just hate it when he is right. "God. This is so fucked up."

"Listen"—Pierce clasps me on the shoulder—"I won't tell anyone. I'll even keep it from Charlotte, which she won't like, but you need to figure out what's going to happen. Because I can tell you have feelings for her."

"When did you become so observant?"

He gives me a smug look. "From one bloke in love to another, it's easy to tell."

I hate it. I hate that he can see right through me. "Is it that obvious?"

"'Fraid so."

"Why are you two out here?" Nash yells from the door of the bar.

"I needed some fresh air," Pierce shouts back. "We're coming."

Nash disappears back inside the bar.

"I'm here if you need me, Simon." Pierce falls into step beside me.

"Appreciate it."

Nothing about this conversation makes me feel better. If anything, it makes me feel worse.

Because no matter which way I try to spin it in my head, the wedding is this week and then I'll be back home. Charade over.

And I have no idea how to make this thing with Layla work.

Fucking real feelings are involved. If only they could've been fake too.

Chapter Twenty-Four

LAYLA

Nerves are swirling in my belly. This is the day I've been dreading.

The fateful town council meeting.

And I'm here by myself.

Simon was needed at the ranch for a potential security issue. I can't fault him for being there. I just hate that I didn't even get to see him last night because of Blake's bachelor party.

Thankfully, he helped me rehearse my speech before he left.

I only wish he were here with me now. Because this is the reason that we're even together.

Watching everyone file in and take their seats, I smooth a hand down the front of my suit jacket.

I didn't want to take any chances. The black felt drab, but hopefully it will impress the town council.

"Layla. How are you today?" Mrs. Bush asks, handing me a copy of the agenda. Her thick, cat-eye glasses make her eyes the size of saucers.

"I'm well. How are you doing?" My voice is syrupy

sweet. I don't want to give these people any ammunition to use against me.

"Fine." She pushes her glasses farther up her nose. "You'll notice you're second on the discussion list this evening."

"Thank you."

I take a seat toward the front, studying every single person on the town council. Most of the council members are older. They're people I remember from my childhood. With Gramps being so active in Dixon, we knew everyone.

And I hate the judging looks they're giving me.

These people know me. They know what kind of person I am. I hate that it's even up for discussion right now.

"Welcome everyone to the town council meeting. We have a few items to address, and then we will open the floor to any concerns from citizens."

Brad's eyes drift across the room, settling on me, before going back to the agenda at hand. He waxes poetic about some new business that is supposedly coming into town. Having to deal with him in order to run my business has always been one of the downsides of Pinstripes & Push-Ups.

But it's my dream. If I have to deal with this asshat every few months, so be it.

Brad nods to Mrs. Bush, who clears her throat.

"Next item on the agenda is the future of Pinstripes & Push-Ups." I hate how excited Mrs. Bush sounds. Brad is sitting next to her, a flat look on his face. "We are going to hear from the owner, Layla Winchester."

Wiping my hands on my pants, I stand up and approach the microphone standing in the center of rows of chairs.

"For those of you who don't know me, I'm Layla

Winchester. I have lived in Dixon my entire life. I love this town. I knew I wanted to give back to my community here. Pinstripes & Push-Ups has been a part of this town for years. Whether it's Dixonites coming in or tourists, every person is welcome at my store."

I clear my throat, and look at each council member sitting at the table in front of me. Some look bored. Some are shifting through the papers in front of them. Others, like Mrs. Bush, look like their minds have already been made up.

I steel my spine. Surely they have to see reason, right?

"I provide jobs for people in town. I attend all the town council meetings. I donate to charities in town and pay my taxes and rent on time. This business has been my dream for as long as I can remember." My voice starts to crack. "I love being able to create for the people of this town. I love seeing the faces of everyone when they leave, feeling better about themselves. I hope you can see the contribution I make to this town and will allow Pinstripes & Push-Ups to continue thriving in this community."

A few people clap as I finish my speech.

"You sell lingerie." Mrs. Bush's lips are pulled into a thin line. So thin, they look like one straight orange lipstick thread. "Your bedroom activities do not need to be thrown in everyone's faces."

The disdain dripping from her voice makes it sound like I'm parading around town naked.

"My bedroom activities?" Is this really what they think of my store? "It helps women feel empowered. That no matter your shape or size, you can feel beautiful. Because you are."

"And that's a reason to showcase *bras* in your window?" She says it like it's a dirty word.

"Among other things." I don't lie. It wouldn't do me

any good right now. "I also support other small businesses by selling their pieces in my store. I believe in lifting everyone up."

"Except not everyone can shop in your store," Brad pipes up.

"Who can't shop there?" I cross my arms, starting to get defensive. It seems that no matter what I do, no one here is going to listen to me.

"Men."

Don't roll your eyes, Layla.

"Men make up almost forty percent of my customers."

"And how do you know this?" Mrs. Bush asks.

"I track business patterns to know what my customers want."

"More like they can't control themselves and have to come in and ogle your store."

There are whispers and murmurs around the room now. I try to steer the meeting back to safer ground. "I know the percentage of my customers because men come in and shop for their wives and girlfriends. I like knowing what they want to buy and catering my business to them."

"So you can sell them lingerie," she clips out, shaking her head.

My patience snaps. "It's not a strip club!"

"That's enough!" Brad intervenes.

You could hear a pin drop in the room it's so quiet. Everyone looks horrified at my words. Why does this woman have the power to stoke the anger simmering inside of me?

I know what my business means to people in this town. I only hope the rest of them do.

"Layla. You are excused from the meeting."

"I'm sorry?" I didn't hear her right.

"We've noted the reasons why you would like your

store to remain in town. But we do not need you here to stir everyone up."

"Stir them up? You've got to be kidding me," I mumble to myself. "If you're making a decision about my business, I have a right to be here."

"You do not need to be present for the vote. Now,"— Mrs. Bush stands, trying to show her assumed power— "you can leave or we can have you escorted out."

I have no doubt that it would be the highlight of her life to throw me out of the meeting.

What a hag.

"Fine. I'll leave. But I hope the council will see the good I do for Dixon when making their decision."

I spin on my heel and walk out of the hall.

I was hoping reason would win out tonight, but I guess not. Tears wet my cheeks as I walk home.

People are spilling out of the Dixon Bar and Grill on this beautiful night. My entire future is on the line as the moon hangs high in the sky.

God, how did it even come down to this?

I wish Simon were here. I need his strength more than I care to admit. If it weren't for him, I don't think we'd have even gotten to this point tonight.

I only hope that everything we've done will bring us the results we want.

Otherwise, what the hell did I rope Simon into?

"Where's your better half today?" Charlotte asks me.

"He had to meet with the lads, he said."

I sip on my champagne.

Today is the last event before the rehearsal dinner tonight. One of the last times I'll get to spend with Simon.

He's been scarce these last few days. Claiming he has to make sure security is tight for the wedding.

With how it's been up until now, it seems excessive. There hasn't been one sighting of anyone who shouldn't be here. No paparazzi at all.

"Well, you look fetching in this outfit, dear." Charlotte waves a hand in front of my outfit. "Hopefully he'll be here to see it."

Blake and Gemma wanted a fun afternoon—complete with dressing up to play croquet. I never turn down a chance to look nice.

With the only requirement being to wear white, I dug out a white bodysuit to pair with a white, tulle skirt.

"You don't look so bad yourself." She's in the pinstripe

jumpsuit that I made for the store. True to her word, she's been back several times to go shopping on her own.

Each time she stops by, she mentions how we can hang out in London when I come and visit Simon. I can only smile and nod.

Because there will be no doing anything together on trips to see my fiancé. No flitting off to England to visit anyone there. If all goes according to plan, I'll have saved my store and can try to expand even further online.

"Well, well, well. What do we have here?" Simon's voice startles me.

"You're here."

"Hi, love." Simon drops a quick kiss on my cheek.

"Everything okay?"

"Fine." He stares ahead.

It's hard to get a read on him. Normally those green eyes of his are so expressive. Today they are hidden behind dark sunglasses.

"You look nice." I let my eyes slide over him. Even though he's not in all white, he looks as sexy as ever in the white button-up and suspenders.

Who knew suspenders could be so hot?

"Not as good as you." He fingers the material of my skirt. "Too bad we're not closer to the pool."

"If you throw me into the pool wearing this, Belvy, I will—"

"You'll what?"

There's that smile I love so much.

I step closer, leaning up so my mouth is right against his ear. "I won't put out tonight."

His growl is low and deep, hitting me in all the right spots. "I guess I can't do that, now can I?"

"Then how about you give me a better kiss?"

"Better, hmm?" Grabbing me around the waist, Simon

hauls me into him. My body is flush against his. "I guess I can make the sacrifice to give you a proper kiss."

His lips slant over mine, igniting my body. As his fingers dig into my side, I open, welcoming his tongue.

I don't know if I'll ever get used to this feeling that he sets off in me. I could kiss him endlessly and it still wouldn't be enough.

But a throat clearing has Simon pulling back. I don't have to see his eyes to know they are lit up with lust and want.

I'm ready to say forget this event and drag him back to his room to have my way with him.

"Better?" Simon drags his nose against mine.

"Better." My voice is a whisper.

"How is it fair that we're playing croquet? Don't British people do this all the time?" Mason's whines distract me from the man whose arms I'm in.

"You sound like Willow. It's a game. You'll do fine," Ivy tells him.

"It's not the eighteen-fifties, Mason. We don't picnic and promenade all day," Sean yells from where he's standing at the starting picket. "Some of us have day jobs."

"You nervous?" Simon asks. "Don't think you can win?"

Mason takes a few steps closer to Simon. Their eyes are locked on one another.

"Want to make a bet of it, Winchester?"

"Oh Lord." I roll my eyes.

"Does Mason even know how to play croquet?" I ask Ivy, who's made her way over to me.

"No.

"How 'bout loser buys drinks. At The Tipsy Cocktail."

"Oh no. Has to be at a neutral site. You can't buy us drinks from your own bar," Simon points out.

"You're assuming I'm going to lose." Mason sounds as cocky as ever.

"Have you ever played before?"

Simon and Mason are going back and forth, ignoring the groups that have already started to play.

"Well, no. But I should pick it up easy enough."

"Fine." Simon sticks his hand out to Mason. "Loser buys drinks at the Dixon Bar and Grill."

"You're on." Mason gives his hand an extra squeeze before dropping it and heading back to Ivy.

"You know how to play, right?" Simon asks.

"It's croquet. I'm pretty sure all we did was knock the balls around when we were kids."

That stops him short. "Knocking balls, love?"

"Head out of the gutter, Belvy. Especially if you want to win this thing."

"Are you any good at this?" Simons asks.

"Are *you* any good at this?" I throw back at him.

"Am I supposed to know how to play since I'm British?"

I elbow him in the side. "I guess we'll get through this together."

"Kiss for luck?" Simon puckers up.

"Well, if it's for luck."

Returning his kiss, we're next up to start. Grabbing a mallet, Simon points where I need to go and I whack it.

It bounces and rolls its way toward the hoop on the far side of the field.

Simon whistles. "Not bad. You taking out some aggression?"

Facing him, I walk backward as Mason and Ivy are up next. "I don't know. Did you do something to warrant it?"

The smile drops off his face immediately. Ice slides through me.

"What's wrong?" I grab his arm.

"Nothing. Stressed about the big day."

It's a lie if I've ever heard one.

"Talk to me, Simon. If something's wrong, let me help."

He blows out a breath before we're being yelled at.

"Get moving you two! You're blocking it for the rest of us!" Mason's shouts startle both of us.

"Nothing to worry about, love." Simon drops a kiss on my cheek before getting out of Mason's way.

The rest of the game goes by in a blur. Mason and Simon keep trash-talking, but it does nothing to settle my thoughts. My brain is racing. Simon's been off all afternoon and it's driving me crazy because I don't know why.

"Alright, love. Game is on the line." Simon stands behind me as I line up my shot. "Hit the stake and we win."

"And Mason has to miss."

Simons laughs. "That too. You've got this, love."

Pushing down all my worrisome thoughts, I hit the ball. Right into the stake.

"Yes!" Simon grabs me, holding me in the air. Laughter bubbles out of both of us. "Take that!"

"You haven't won yet." Mason's ball goes sailing past the stake, sealing our victory.

"Yes! Now we did!"

I leap into Simon's waiting arms. He spins me around, planting a loud smack on my lips.

"Brilliant, love."

There's a sadness to his voice as he plays with a stray lock of hair.

"You sure you're okay?"

"Fine. Distracted, is all.

"I guess drinks are on me." Mason walks over, extending his hand to Simon.

"Good match."

Mason drops his hand and wraps me in a quick hug. "I like him, sis. You found a good one. Even if he beat me."

"Thanks." I try to swallow around the sudden lump in my throat.

I don't want to let Simon go, but I don't know how to keep him. He leaves in three days. Three days and he'll be gone from my life.

I knew I shouldn't have done this. It was stupid to think that I could escape this unscathed.

Because I've gone and done the one thing I didn't think I would do.

Fall in love with my fake fiancé.

By the time this ends, everything should work out for the best. I'll still have my store, maybe even be able to grow my business, and this will have all been worth it.

If I keep telling myself that, maybe I'll start to believe it. All I want now is Simon. The man who stepped up to help me without question. Who cares for me in a way I've never felt from a man before.

Everything he does, he does for me.

If only our lives weren't on two different continents. There's no way this will work with almost five thousand miles separating us.

"I'll pick you up tonight before the rehearsal?" Simon asks quietly.

I nod, biting on my lip to keep myself in check. "I'll see you then."

My heart and mind are spinning out of control, trying to cling to anything that is real. Because if I keep focusing on Simon leaving, I'll spiral.

Now, if only I can keep my emotions in check until Monday.

Three days.

I can fall apart after he leaves and takes my heart with him.

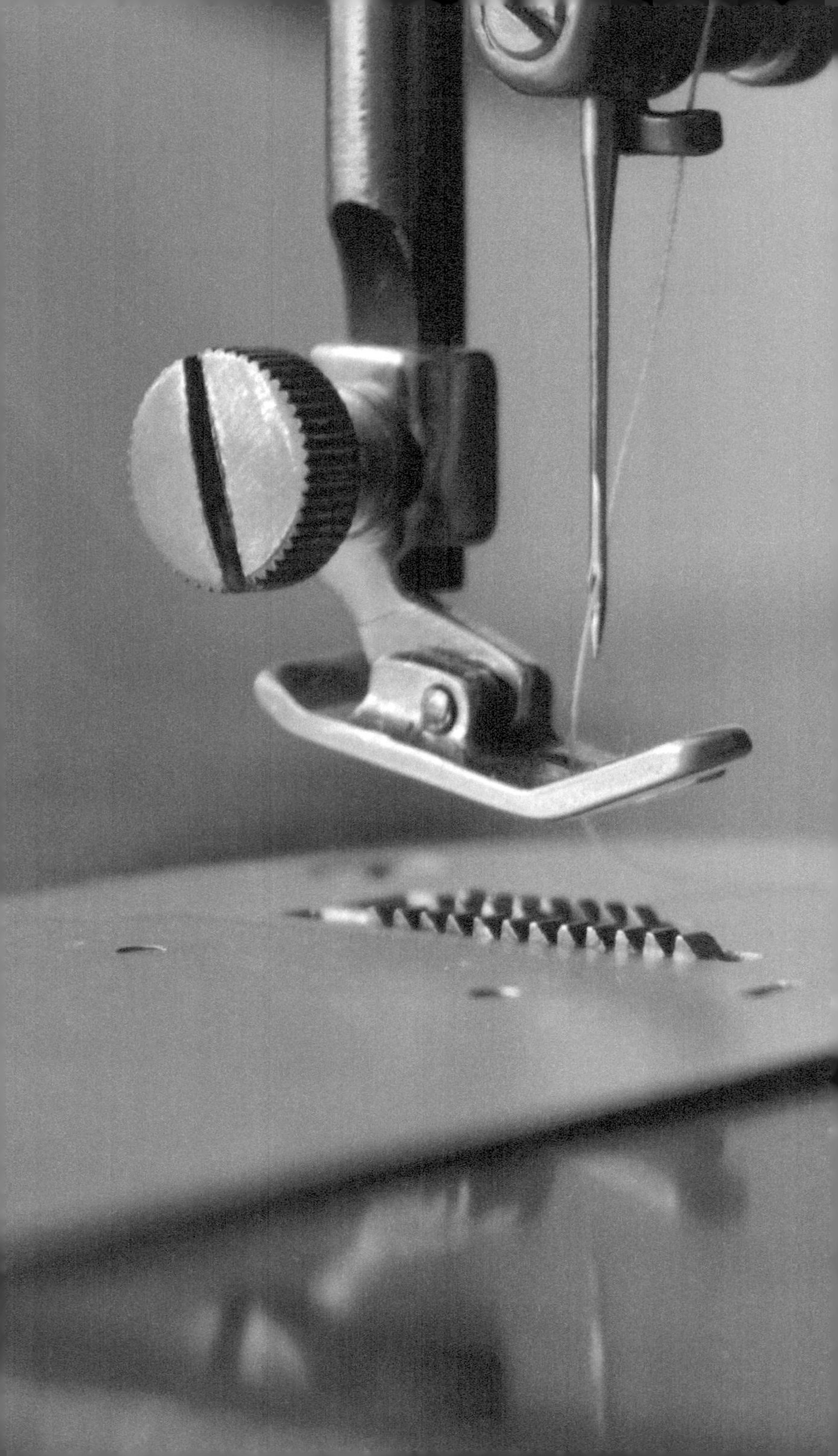

Chapter Twenty-Six

LAYLA

Big smile, Layla, big smile.

Swiping a final coat of lip gloss over my mouth, I give myself one last once-over in the mirror. I smooth my hands down the black chiffon fabric of my dress. The deep V of the top highlights all my best features. It's subtle, yet simple. Not taking away from my sister on the night of her rehearsal dinner.

And one of the last few nights I have with Simon.

Big smile, Layla.

Not matter how much I try to tell myself this, an ache has settled inside my chest. Deep under my heart, it feels like it will never go away.

Simon will be leaving on Monday. I don't even know if it hurt this much when I left Brad. I was a shell of who I was when I left him. With Simon? I've never felt more like myself.

I don't know what's going to happen when Simon leaves.

A knock on my door draws my attention away from my morose thoughts.

Crossing the empty living room, I open the door. The man consuming my every thought eats up every bit of space in the entry way.

In a black suit with a white shirt that's left unbuttoned, scruff lining his jaw, Simon looks delicious.

"Layla, love. You look fucking gorgeous."

Strong hands wrap around my waist, pulling me into him. The strong tea and lemon scent wafts over me. It sends butterflies exploding in my belly. My core clenches at the thought of getting to be wrapped up in this man all night long.

One of the last few nights with him.

I push that thought away, not wanting to focus on it right now.

"You, Mr. Belvy, look pretty damn good yourself."

"Yeah?" He tips my chin up to meet his gaze. "Not as good as you."

He drags a single finger down my chest, pulling ever so gently at the bunching of the fabric under my breasts.

"Yes, well, it'd be hard for you to pull off a dress like this."

Simon's smile is downright sinful as he pulls me close. His breath ghosts over my lips.

"It'll be damn easy to pull this dress off you later tonight."

His lips capture mine in a fiery kiss. My fingers dig into his chest, wanting to keep this man as close as possible to me.

"We need to go," Simon growls, pulling back.

"Go where?" It's like Simon has taken every thought and swirled it around. I can't think clearly when he's around.

"To the rehearsal dinner."

"Right." I shake my head, trying to clear the fog this

man has been inducing for the last month any time he's near me. "Dinner. Then we can go back to your place."

"My place?" Simon wipes his thumb under my lips. No doubt wiping away any evidence of that kiss.

I nod. "It's a short walk as opposed to a thirty minute ride through town. And I want to have my way with you tonight. While I still can."

"Right."

A bucket of ice is thrown over us. I hate that I pulled us back to the present.

We've been living in our own little bubble.

I don't know when this fake thing turned into something real. But it's more real than anything I've ever experienced.

"We better get going."

Simon links his hand with mine and pulls me out the door behind him. Downtown Dixon is bustling with tourists as Simon helps me into the truck and we head toward the ranch.

The ride over is quiet. It seems both of us are lost in our thoughts.

Back when this whole thing started, I figured it'd be easy to play off our broken engagement. Simon in London and me here with the distance too hard to overcome.

Now, it seems an impossible wall to climb over.

My entire life is in Dixon. My store, my family. Everything.

And Simon? Simon's entire life is in London. Thousands of miles apart and I have no idea how this could even begin to work.

Before I know it, Simon is pulling the truck into the ranch. It's buzzing with excitement.

"Ready?" Simon asks as he opens my door.

No. But that doesn't mean it's going to make these next few days slow down.

"Let's go." I paste on a bright smile as we follow the music to the barn.

Simon pulls me in close, whispering in my ear, "Did you think we'd be here after you accused me of trying to crash the wedding?"

That puts a genuine smile on my face. "I'm surprised you even talked to me after that. Can you blame me though? Who comes into a barn wearing an all-black suit?"

"Private security," he says with a straight face.

"Yes, I'll remember that next time I happen to run into one of you in the barn."

"Layla!" Gemma rushes up to us. "You look gorgeous."

I hug my sister tight to me. "Not as gorgeous as you."

"Thanks to you." She spins. "Can you believe she made this, Simon?"

"I can. Layla is very talented." He squeezes my hip.

The dress I made for Gemma tonight is beautiful. The soft white lace fabric hugs her curves. It hits just above her knees. Tasteful, but simple. It's her beaming smile that lights her up from the inside out.

It's the look of love.

"That she is." Gemma leans up, giving him a peck on the cheek.

"You look great," he tells her. "Everything does."

The ranch is done up to the nines. Two long tables are spread out underneath string lights that hang from the rafters. Flowers and candles fill the space, as waiters move between the guests delivering drinks and hors d'oeuvres.

With the actual rehearsal having taken place earlier in the day, the evening is a laid-back affair with dinner and drinks.

Simon gets pulled off to talk with Sean and Pierce while I mingle with out-of-town family members I haven't seen in a few years.

The excitement for Gemma and Blake's big day is palpable. It's hard to believe that after a month of events, the wedding is tomorrow. Gemma and Blake opened the dinner to everyone from town, wanting to include them in the celebrations not just tomorrow, but tonight too.

"Layla."

I fight the groan. Of course the last person I want to deal with tonight is here.

"Brad. What are you doing here?"

Mrs. Bush is standing next to him, a delighted smile on her face. Not something I am used to seeing from her.

"I was hoping to speak to you about Pinstripes & Push-Ups."

"Now?" I hiss at him, dragging him away from the crowds. "It's my sister's rehearsal dinner."

I've been trying to meet with this prick all summer and he chooses now to talk to me about it?

His face is smarmy. I can't fucking stand it. "Time was of the essence, so I figured you wouldn't mind."

A few eyes are starting to dart our way. No doubt they want to see if anything happens between me and my ex.

"Fine. What is it?" I cross my arms, trying to look as disinterested as possible in this conversation. I don't want to give these two any more leverage over me than they already have.

Mrs. Bush pulls out a piece of paper from a folder in her hand. My eyes skim over it, but they catch on the one sentence that is the most important. *Permits have been revoked for the property and the business will cease to operate at its current location.*

"I'm sorry, what in the hell is this?" I flash the paper in front of her face.

"Now, Layla. Please don't make a scene," she tells me.

"Then maybe you shouldn't have told me you're closing my store at my sister's rehearsal dinner!" I shout.

"Layla." Brad grabs my elbow to pull me away from the crowd, but I shrug him off.

"Don't touch me." I'm fuming. Enraged. Angrier than I ever remember being in my entire life. "Why in the hell are you doing this?"

"Layla, dear. We can't have someone of such immoral character running a store here. What would that tell people who come to visit?"

"Immoral character? For God's sake. It's clothing and lingerie. I'm not selling devil worshipping accessories."

Mrs. Bush gasps in shock. Apparently that's what she equates lingerie to being.

"More to do with you lying to everyone," Brad says.

"What?"

That stops me.

"It's come to my attention that your relationship status might not be what you say it is."

My mouth goes dry. How in the world could Brad possibly know that Simon isn't actually my fiancé?

"Did you really think you'd get away with it? Hiring someone to be your fiancé?" Mrs. Bush chimes in. "Really, Layla. It's a disgrace to the entire town."

It's a punch to the stomach. I've done nothing but try to be the perfect person that these people want. An upstanding store owner. Someone the town would be proud to have as part of their business community.

But it makes absolutely no difference. I now realize that no matter what I did, they were going to close down my store. They never wanted it, and what the mayor wants, the mayor gets.

"You'll have until the end of—"

I cut Mrs. Bush off. I don't want to hear whatever she has to say. It's only going to stoke the anger that is now swirling in my gut.

"Save it. I don't want to hear any of it." As my anger grows, so does my voice. I ignore all the eyes I feel on me.

"Layla, keep your voice down." Brad looks around. He was never one for being in the center of conflict.

Why he chose to go into politics, I don't know.

"I will not keep my voice down. I am sick and tired of everyone in this town dictating what I do and don't do. I'm done. Take my store. You were never going to let me keep it anyway."

I shove the paper back in Brad's chest.

"See? This is why we can't have someone so dramatic running a store," Mrs. Bush whispers to Brad.

As I turn to leave, it's then I notice no one is speaking. Every single eye in the barn is focused on me.

A burning humiliation creeps through me.

No one was supposed to find out about this. How Brad did, I don't know. Harsh stares and disapproving looks face me.

I can't take this. Pushing through the crowds in the barn, I burst out the doors. I find the well-trod path into the woods behind the lodge and leave the party behind me.

Everything is coming undone. In the blink of an eye, everything I've been working for is gone. All because of a few people who don't approve of what I do.

My chest is tight, thinking about what happened back there. I don't know how I'm going to face all those people, my family—Gemma—when I have to go back.

I lied, and there's no other way around it.

"Are you alright?" Simon's voice is soft, carrying like a wisp through the warm summer night.

"No." I wrap my arms around myself, trying to quell all the emotions. My voice wavers, giving me away.

"Layla." His hand lands on my shoulder turning to face him, but I shrug it off. "Talk to me, love."

Love. That damn nickname that made me swoon.

Now it's a knife to the heart.

"What's there to say? Somehow Brad found out about us, and now my store is gone."

"Shit." A remorseful look comes over his face. "Layla, look—"

A mirthless laugh escapes, cutting him off. "Of course this would all come unraveling so close to the end."

"But that can't be it." Simon takes a step toward me, but I take a step back. Right now, I don't think there's anyone that can comfort me.

"Seems pretty final to me. This was always going to end, Simon. It just blew up in our faces so why keep fighting? It's done. Over."

I'm a ball of emotions, and I have no idea which emotion is winning. Except a frustrated, angry tear slips out.

"You're serious." It's not a question. It's almost like he knows. Now that the cat is out of the bag, there's no reason to continue this.

"What's the point?" Locking eyes with him, his pain matches mine. "I live here. You're in London. We always knew this thing would end as soon as you went back home."

"You're going to let those wankers dictate the rest of your life?"

"It's not like I can keep fighting back. I'm tired, Simon. I'm done. Just done."

"That's not the girl I know."

"Then maybe you really didn't know me. It's not like this was real. We were never going to beat them." I brush away another tear.

"Not real?" Simon closes the distance between us, pulling me into his arms. "Fuck that, Layla. This was never fake. It's been real since the day we met."

"It's never been real for me, Simon."

The lie cuts deep. But on Monday, Simon will be out of my life for good. There's no point in keeping this charade going.

"You're taking the easy way out, Layla." There's a bite to his tone. "I didn't think you'd give up this easy."

"It's called self-preservation." I step out of his hold, turning my back to him. It's better this way. Not looking at him.

"Call it whatever you want, but it's not the woman I fell in love with."

"What?"

Simon is gone, his shoulders hunched as he jogs down the trail.

"Fuck."

More tears escape. Ever since I left Brad, I've kept my walls high. I never wanted to feel like that again. To lose myself. To not recognize the girl in the mirror.

No one ever attempted to scale them. I never bothered to even try with some guys.

Yet, with one visit to Dixon, I let Simon in. He's the only person who showed himself worthy. No, proved himself worthy.

No one ever cared enough to try before. And now?

Now, it turns out I lost myself to the one man who was never mine to begin with.

Chapter Twenty-Seven

LAYLA

"Tell me it's not true."

Erica bursts in through the back door of the shop. With the wedding in just a few short hours, I closed the store today. Nothing is more important than Gemma's big day.

Even if my entire world is coming apart at the seams.

A closure that will be permanent, if the notice on the front door this morning is anything to go on.

"I guess bad news travels fast."

"They're really closing Pinstripes & Push-Ups?"

I look around at all the white silk that is strewn across my workroom. Half-finished pieces hang on mannequins. Beautiful works of art that the town of Dixon decided they don't want here anymore.

"They are." I hand her the notice that greeted me this morning. A bright orange sign that sealed my fate. "We only have a few days to get out."

"You can't let them do this!" Her voice borders on shrieking.

"It's done."

"Is it though? You have to fight this."

Last night, I might have agreed with her. Anger warred with sadness mixed with hurt. But watching Simon's retreating form? It's like he took any and all fight I had with him.

"And what about next week when they think that the newest top I design is too risqué?" I shake my head. "I can't keep going around and around with the town leaders on this."

"What will you do?"

"I don't know."

The question has been nagging at me. This shop is everything. Everything I've wanted to do for as long as I can remember.

Designing clothes.

Helping people feel beautiful in something I make.

One dumb decision—trying to save my business with Simon's help—and it's gone.

The ache in my chest swells. Not only have I lost my dream, but I've lost Simon too. How could I let the most amazing man in my life walk away?

I was up all night thinking about him. I don't even think I was this broken up when I left Brad. Simon leaving cut deep. Deeper than I ever expected a fake fiancé to hurt.

"We need to talk." This time, it's Gemma bursting into my studio.

"What are you doing here?" Glancing down at my watch, I should be leaving to head to the ranch to get hair and makeup done. Yet, the woman of the hour is standing in my shop, looking none too pleased with me.

"Erica, will you give me a minute with my sister?"

"Sure." She heads out the front, the door slamming shut behind her.

"What in the hell is wrong with you?" Gemma's brown eyes are fierce.

"Do we really have to talk about this today? Aren't there more important things going on?"

"No."

It's eerie how calm she is. She's getting married today. On my wedding day, I was a bundle of nerves. Nothing could calm me down. Maybe I should have taken that as a sign I shouldn't have gotten married.

"You and Simon were faking this whole time?"

"Yes, but——"

"Why didn't you tell me?" she explodes. I've never seen my sister this angry with me. "I deserved to know!"

"It was your wedding. I wasn't going to do anything to take the focus off you."

"And yet, here we are, Layla."

"Damn it." Standing, I approach my sister like a baby deer. I don't want to spook her—or piss her off even more. "I'm sorry, okay? I didn't want this to happen."

She waves me off. "I don't care about the focus not being on me. I care that you didn't feel like you could tell me any of this was going on. You know I've always got your back, Layla."

The pain in my heart grows. No matter what I seem to do lately, I keep disappointing everyone around me.

Erica.

Simon.

Gemma.

The entire fucking town.

"What was I supposed to say? 'Hey, Gem. The town things I'm a harlot because I'm single and design my own lingerie, and to get them off my back Simon is going to pretend to date me because it looks better? Oh, but wait, I accidentally said we were getting married because the old bats couldn't handle a single woman being successful in her own right.'"

My breath leaves me in a rush. When I brave the courage to look at Gemma, she's smiling.

"Since when do you care what everyone in town thinks?"

"Since it could ruin my business." The *duh* is implied.

"Are they really going to shut you down?" she asks.

"Yup." The p pops off my tongue. I toss the notice at her. "It's official."

"And you're going to let this be the end of Pinstripes & Push-Ups?" She crumples up the paper and tosses it into the overflowing trash.

It's a never-ending cycle. First with Erica and now with Gemma. "What am I supposed to do? I need a store to sell my clothes."

She waves me off. "This isn't the Layla I know."

"Oh yeah? Who is the Layla you know?" Crossing my arms, I sink back into my chair.

Gemma comes up and grabs my hands. "The Layla I know is a badass. She wouldn't let someone like that douchebag, Brad, and Mrs. Bush stop you from going after what you really want. So you lost the store? Big deal. There's other ways to sell things these days. The Layla I know wouldn't go down without a fight."

Tears well in my eyes at her words.

"And what about the other…situation?"

I don't know how else to word it.

"Simon? It's all fake, right?" Her question is leading.

Did it start out as fake? Yes.

Until my cat made the first move. Now I can't imagine my life without him.

"He's leaving Monday. It doesn't matter."

"You love him."

Hot, fat drops of tears start running down my face at her words.

I love Simon. I love him more than I ever thought I could love anyone. Who cares if we only knew each other for a few weeks?

What we had was real. One of the most real things I've ever had in my life.

Gemma walks over, wrapping her arms around me.

"We can fix this."

A watery laugh escapes. "Don't we need to be leaving to get ready?" I mumble into her hair.

"They can wait. Blake's mom will be pissed, but I don't care." Gemma squeezes me even tighter. "There has to be a way we can make this right. Your store and Simon."

I pull back, wiping the tears from my face. "Why don't we worry about getting you married first?"

Her smile is as bright as I've ever seen it.

At least one of us will get our happy ending.

Chapter Twenty-Eight

SIMON

"You're looking blue." Pierce says by way of greeting.

"Fuck off, mate."

I'm exhausted. After the chaos of the rehearsal dinner last night, I didn't sleep a wink. The only thing my mind could focus on was the look of dejection on Layla's face when everyone found out this thing between us was fake. A ruse for her to keep her shop.

I can't believe I fucked up.

"Really. You don't look good."

"Pierce, I'm really not in the mood."

"Sorry. Need a drink?" He motions to the small selection of drinks sitting on top of the dresser.

"I'm good. Want to stay clearheaded for today."

Even though all I want to do is drown my sorrows right now.

"I'm sorry about how things went down last night." Pierce looks sad. Probably one of the only few times I've seen him that way. "How'd they find out?"

"Beats the fuck out of me."

"Do you think it was Brad?"

"If it was, that would mean I fucked up."

And ruined everything for Layla. The one thing we said was we wouldn't tell anyone.

Somewhere along the way, this thing with her went from fake to real. More real than anything I've ever experienced.

I've never met someone like her. She's strong. She's fierce. She didn't back down from this town telling her they didn't want her.

Look how well that turned out.

I don't know who I'm more pissed at. Me for letting it slip or this town for turning their backs on one of their own.

My radio crackles to life.

"Boss. We've got a live one."

With the wedding today, I didn't want to take any chances for security and have every man on duty. Just what I need this morning.

"What sector?"

"Seven."

I slide the radio back into my pocket.

"Everything okay?" Pierce asks.

"Need to check things out. Stay here."

Rushing out of their suite, I head to find the golf cart to take me to the far edge of the property. With guests due to arrive at any minute, I want to get whatever this is taken care of away from prying eyes.

My guy has someone sitting with his back to the tree. From what I can tell, they are arguing about something.

As soon as I park the golf cart, both sets of eyes are on me. Stretching myself out of the cart, the guy on the ground looks scared.

Good.

At least I know I'm doing one thing right.

"What's going on over here?"

I cross my arms, making sure to flex my biceps to look even more menacing.

"Found him climbing over the fence."

"You know you're trespassing on private property, right?"

With the ranch being so large, I don't think the press knows what's Winchester land and what's not. But given the camera around his neck, I'd say he knows what he's doing.

"Look man, can't you just let me go?"

The guy looks sleazy. With a ponytail hanging down his back and a grungy leather jacket, he isn't doing much to try and fit in.

"Won't be happening."

"Do you know how much a photo of Tiffany Travers at her son's wedding would go for?" he argues.

This is who he wanted a picture of? Blake's mom?

Idiot.

"Christ. Get him out of here."

"What do you want me to do with him?" my guy asks.

I study the man with a camera around his neck. "Take him down to the police station. Let him wait the wedding out there and then they can release him."

"Oh c'mon, man. Just one picture."

"No. And you're lucky we aren't pressing charges."

I'm shocked it took this long for a journalist to make a move. And for it not to be for Charlotte or Ellie, but Blake's mom? That is a surprise. Clearly the guy isn't from England because a shot of Charlotte or Ellie would've gotten him a lot more.

At least I know my men are on top of it.

I take my time getting back to the main lodge. It's not like I have anything to rush back to. Walking away from Layla last night had been the last thing I wanted to do.

But when Brad and Mrs. Bush—fucking wankers—blew everything up, they took the woman I knew with them.

The Layla I know wouldn't have backed down like that. Hell, maybe I never knew her at all.

Guests are starting to make their way back to the where the ceremony will be held. Pierce and Charlotte are sitting on the wraparound porch watching their kids play with their cousins.

"Is this what you two are going to look like in your old age?" The porch creeks under my weight as I cross over to where they are.

Pierce kisses the back of Charlotte's hand. "I don't know, mate. I wouldn't mind spending more time out here."

"We won't be bringing Simon back, that's for sure," Charlotte mutters.

"What was that?" I stick my ear closer to her.

I heard every word she said.

"I'm mad at you," Charlotte hisses. She looks as lovely as she always does, dressed in a soft blue dress with a tie around the neck. It's something I've seen her wear before. "How could you lie to us?"

"We didn't want to. But I would do it again to help Layla."

"Holy shit."

"What?"

Charlotte pins me with a fierce stare.

"You love her."

"Hey!" Pierce chimes in. "I already told you that."

"You can be a bit daft sometimes on love, my dear. I love you, but I had to see it for myself."

"I was right though."

"Aww, do you want a biscuit?" I ask him.

"Biscuits? Can we have some?" Jane pops her head up from where she's playing in the yard. "Please, Mummy?"

"There will be cupcakes later. Maybe if you're good, I'll let you have two."

"Yes!"

"Back to the point. You love Layla," Charlotte tells me.

"Correct."

"And what are you going to do about it?" Charlotte tips one eyebrow up. The look she is giving me is one I don't want to be on the receiving end of.

"What is there to do? Her entire life is here."

"Maybe not," Pierce says.

"That is what you told me the other night. Has it changed?" I try to keep the growing frustration from bubbling over.

Pierce brushes me off. "The store is closed."

"We don't know that. She loves that place. She's not going to want to come to England with me."

Pierce pulls his phone out of his pocket, opens the photos app, and shoves it in my face. There's a big orange 'CLOSED' sign on the front of her store.

Fuck.

"Can they actually do this?" I ask Pierce.

"Fuck if I know. I know nothing about American politics."

I drop down into the chair next to Charlotte, shoving a rough hand through my hair. This is the last thing I want to be talking about right now.

Thinking about Layla only makes the ache in my chest grow.

And seeing her at the wedding when I can't be with her? All eyes will no doubt be on Gemma, but with the way I've seen this town gossip? There'll be some pretty cutting glares thrown Layla's way too.

"Listen, your pride might be wounded now. But is that any reason to give up the person you love?" Charlotte asks.

"Who does Uncle Simon love?" Jane jumps onto Charlotte's lap.

"Aunt Layla."

"She's really pretty. She looks like a princess," she tells me.

"Pierce, will you take her to get her basket for the flowers?"

"What are daddies for?" He lifts Jane into his arms and claps me on the shoulder before getting Mary and heading back to the ceremony site.

"You need a drink."

Charlotte hands me the flask tucked into her purse.

"You know there is an open bar, right?"

It doesn't stop me from taking a swig of the scotch inside.

"I brought it downstairs for you."

I blow out a breath. "Am I really that big of a sad sack right now?"

"You're heartbroken." Charlotte squeezes my arm. "The way I look at it, you have two choices. You can either man up and stay here with her and help her through this, or go crawling back to London like a wanker."

Christ, Pierce has rubbed off on her.

I shake my head, staring out at the mountains beyond. Guests are starting to arrive for the wedding. There's not a cloud in the sky. It's the perfect day for a wedding.

"Can't I just go back home and lick my wounds in peace?"

I don't deserve to be heartbroken when it was my fault

to begin with. We would've spent the night together before she left to help her sister get ready for her wedding.

"I didn't take you for someone who gives up, Belvy," Charlotte says.

A smile tugs at the corner of my mouth, hearing Charlotte call me by my last name just like Layla does.

"If Pierce gave up, where would we be? We wouldn't have two beautiful daughters and be doing exactly what we want in life." Charlotte stands, her heels clacking against the wooden porch. "All hope is not lost."

I knock back another sip of scotch.

The ache in my chest right now feels pretty hopeless.

I love Layla. That's all there is to it. Whether she loves me back or not is a different story. She has wounds in her past that might make even the most optimistic person wary. I've seen it with my mum. Jumping from one bad guy to another. When the right guy finally did come along, she didn't trust herself to know he was the right guy until it was almost too late.

I don't want that for Layla. She's the strongest fucking person I know. Maybe this is just a bump in the road for her. Maybe she'll come back swinging better than ever.

That's all I want for her. I've seen her dream and how passionate she is about it. If she can get that back, that's all that matters.

Even if it's not with me at her side.

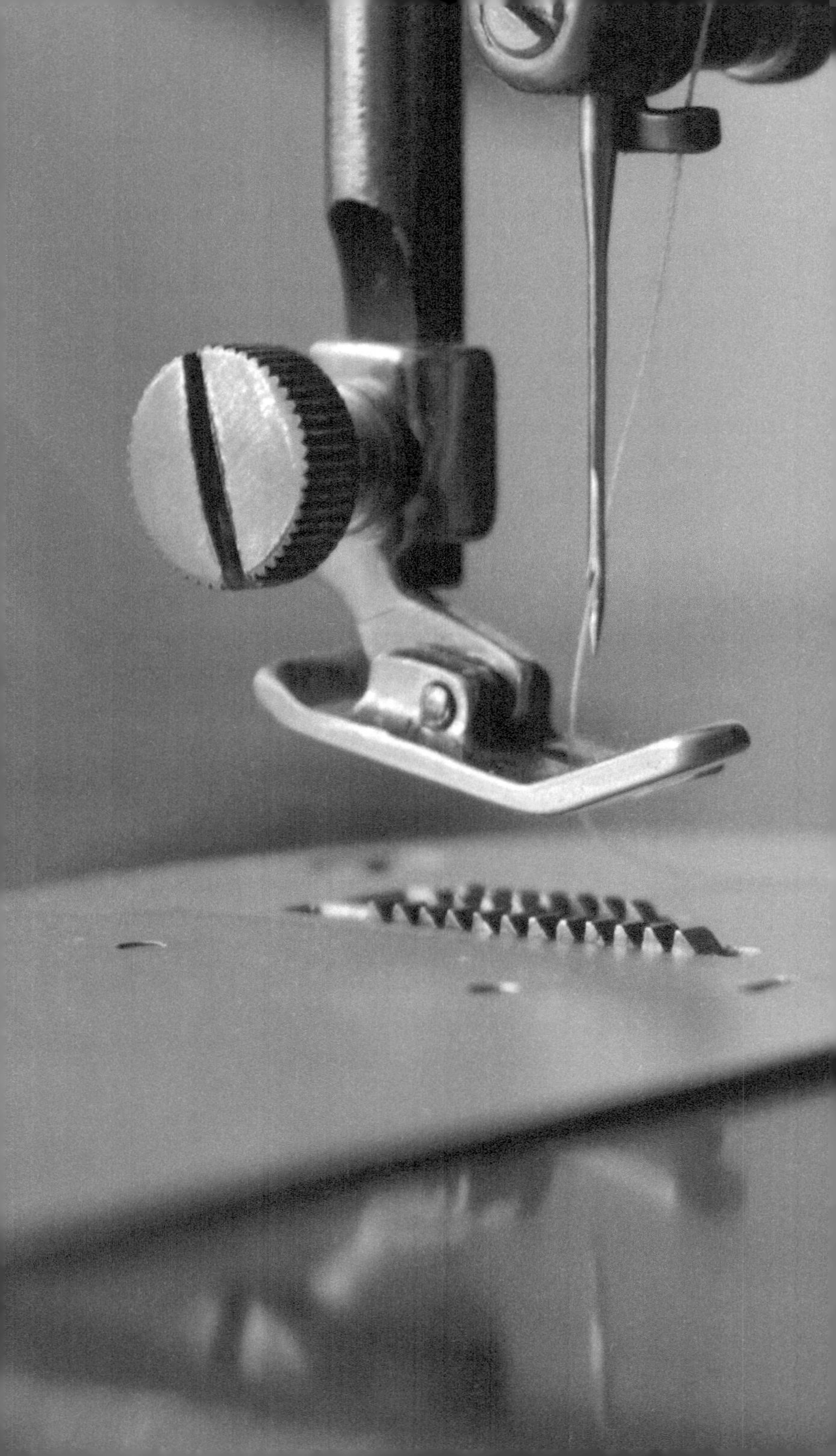

Chapter Twenty-Nine

LAYLA

"You look gorgeous."

"You sure these aren't too much?" Gemma pulls up her dress, showing off her cowboy boots.

Ivy shakes her head. "They're perfect."

"You look really pretty, Aunt Gemma," Willow chimes in.

Gemma's dress might be the most beautiful thing I've ever created. The intricate, floral design wraps around her bust, dipping low—but not too low. Beads and pearls are sewn into the material, shimmering as she moves. The deep V in the back is sexy, giving way to an A-line skirt that hides her boots.

In short, she looks stunning.

"Blake won't know what hit him."

Gemma's eyes get glassy and she turns to me. "Thank you for being by my side today. I know your life isn't exactly rosy right now—"

Pulling her in for a hug, I cut off anything further. "There is no place else I'd be today. You'd have to fight me to keep me from standing up for you today."

"Is it wrong to be nervous?" Gemma whispers so only I can hear. "Now that it's finally here, I feel like I could burst into confetti or throw up."

I laugh, giving her one more squeeze. "I'd be more worried if you weren't nervous. But you and Blake might be one of the most annoyingly loving couples I've met."

"Hey!" she protests. "That's Ivy and Mason." Her voice is loud enough that everyone can hear.

"What about us?" Ivy asks, straightening out Willow's flower girl dress.

"Just how grossly in love you are."

She shakes her head. "Nope, that's you two for sure."

"I agree with Aunt Gemma. You and Dad kiss. Like, a lot." Willow makes a disgusted face.

"See if I sneak you an extra cupcake when your dad isn't looking," Ivy tells her.

"Aunt Gemma is the grossest!" Willow changes her tune immediately, causing all of us to burst out laughing.

Leave it to the eight-year-old to break any tension.

"Are you ready, girls?" Mom peeks her head inside the door. "Oh, sweetheart."

Tears gather in her eyes.

"If you start crying, you'll make me cry, Mom," Gemma chides.

"You are glowing." She crosses the room, wrapping Gemma in a hug.

"Nothing else you want to tell us there, Gem?" Ivy says on a laugh.

"Don't go starting any rumors!"

"Sometimes rumors can be true…"

"Ivy, I'm not pregnant."

She shrugs a shoulder. "I know Willow wants a cousin here."

"And a baby brother!" she pipes up. "I want one of them too!"

Ivy's eyes grow wide. "Keep dreaming, Willow."

"I hate to interrupt this…" Mom trails off, "but everyone is waiting. Are you ready?"

"I'm ready."

Gemma and Mom link their arms together, and we all head out of the lodge. Lights hang from the trees, looking like fairies. Flowers line the path leading to where the ceremony is being held.

It's magical.

Ivy and Willow walk ahead of me as the voices of the crowd start to become louder. I see Dad waiting for Gemma and Mom, then my gaze locks on to the one person I'd rather not see.

Simon is standing in the back. Wearing all-black, he looks sexier than I've ever seen.

What the hell have I done?

His eyes track me as I turn to walk down the aisle. Gramps, Blake, and my brothers are waiting under the archway that Mason built for the wedding.

Every thought should be focused on my sister and Blake, but my mind keeps drifting to Simon. To the man I turned away.

Gramps gives me a smile as I take my place. With the music starting, all eyes are on Gemma.

Except mine. Mine are on the groom. Because tears leak out of Blake's eyes as Gemma gets closer and closer to him.

The look of a man in love.

When Gemma meets him, her tears match his. These two couldn't be more perfect for each other. The way they support each other, love each other, encourage each other…God, it's what I had with Simon.

My mind is all over the place as Gramps's words continue.

"Now, you both have prepared your own vows—"

"Easy for the writer," Gemma says, causing everyone to laugh.

Gramps smiles back at her. "Well then, why don't we hear what he has to say?"

Blake grabs a sheet of paper from his pocket. "Gemma, I don't know how I ever lived without you."

His words to my sister have my tender heart shredding. Listening to him pour out his love for Gemma makes me ache inside. On the happiest day of her life, my own is in tatters.

I can't help but search out Simon. His position has moved, now on the outskirts of the crowd. Almost like he's trying to put as much space between the two of us as he can.

Standing here, on my sister's happiest day, I can't help but be brought back to my own wedding and divorce.

Brad and I were together for seven years. When I left him, I didn't feel like this. Like my heart was ripped from my chest.

All these years after the divorce, I was coasting. Simon brought me back. I did everything for everyone else. Never taking my own wants or needs into account. Being what everyone wanted me to be. The perfect lady with perfect morals who always colored within the lines. And in doing so, I fed exactly into what this town wanted me to be. Going back to the person who bent for everyone else.

But that's not me. I'm not perfect—never have been.

Life is messy and lines get blurred.

Like the one between Simon and me.

This was supposed to be temporary. A means to an end. A way to keep my shop and grow my business. Simon would leave and no one would be any the wiser. We'd quietly end the engagement after a few months.

But Simon walking away from me? I don't think I can handle that. Seeing him at the back of the field, behind all the wedding guests, it feels like a river is between us that I don't know how to cross.

Simon's eyes meet mine, so full of turmoil that it nearly cracks my heart.

How can I ever be done with someone like him? Someone who made me feel safe. Someone who let me be the real me when it was just the two of us. He saw my strengths and my vulnerabilities. With him, I was my most authentic self.

There's no way I can let him go back to London without telling him.

Without telling him—showing him—what he means to me.

Because I don't want to live without Simon.

Gramps's words bring me back to the present.

"I now pronounce you husband and wife. Blake,"—Gramps nods to him—"you may kiss your bride."

The smile on Blake's face could be seen from space as he sweeps Gemma into his arms, giving her the sweetest kiss in front of their family and friends. Cheers and whoops sound out from the crowd.

I wipe the tears from my eyes as she turns back to me, a blush covering her face, as she reaches for her flowers.

"Congratulations, Mrs. Travers." I wrap Gemma in a quick hug before she links arms with Blake and walks back down the aisle, stopping for another kiss at the end.

Taking the best man's arm, I follow her. My eyes go back to where Simon was standing, but he's not there.

What the hell?

Frenzied nerves course through me. Where could

Simon have gone? As soon as we reach the end of the aisle, guests start standing, grabbing champagne from the waiting servers. I grab a glass, needing something to calm my nerves.

If he left…

Simon is standing with Pierce and Charlotte, their little ones running around at their feet. That momentary feeling of panic mixes with the longing in my chest. Swallowing down the rest of my champagne, I stalk over to him.

"We need to talk."

"Now's not really the best time."

"Ouch. That was cold, bro." Pierce slaps him on the shoulder.

This would be easier without them standing right here, but I don't care. I don't want him to leave without hearing what I have to say.

"Five minutes. You can at least give me that."

"In front of everyone?" The guests have left their seats and are mingling around the barn, waiting for the doors to open.

"I don't care!" I shout, louder than necessary. It draws the eyes of people around me. Pierce and Charlotte grab their kids and give us some space. "I am so sick and tired of caring what people in this town think of me, that if I want to tell you I love you, I'm going to!"

Simon looks taken aback. "What's this now?"

Glancing around, I see Gemma and Blake with glasses of champagne, watching me. Gemma gives me an eager thumbs-up, encouraging me.

Closing the distance between the two of us, I've overwhelmed by Simon's scent. That lemon and tea scent—so uniquely British. Uniquely him.

"I lost myself, Simon. After I got divorced, I didn't know who I was. I went so far into a shell to be the woman everyone else wanted me to be, that I forgot who I was. It took a long time for me to find her again. So many people in this town looked down on me. For being single. For owning the business that I do. They didn't think it was 'right' that I made and sold lingerie."

I suck in a breath. Grabbing the lapels of Simon's suit, I pull him closer.

"You never once made me feel less than. Or different. I felt safe to be the real me with you. You signed up for this entire, crazy scheme to help me and you barely knew me."

Simon's lips quirk up. The barest hint of a smile.

That has to be good, right?

"You accepted me as is and I've never felt so safe or loved by anyone in my entire life. I got scared,"—my voice starts to shake—"when I thought I was losing everything."

"And did you? Lose everything?" Simon asks, leaning closer. His hand cups my jaw. The warmth seeps through me, giving me the courage to tell him everything I'm feeling. I've missed his touch more than I ever thought possible.

I shake my head, leaning in to his touch. "No. Because I realized if I have you, I can take on whatever or whoever stands in my way. *Our* way. Because all of this means nothing if I don't have the man I love by my side."

Simon's thumb brushes the apple of my cheek. "There's the girl I fell in love with."

"Yeah?" My breath escapes me in a whoosh.

"Fuck yeah. I love you, Layla." Simon's lips take mine in a soul-stirring kiss. It has every piece of my heart flying back together.

It's the feeling of coming home. Of finding the person who I am meant to spend my life with. It took some bumps and detours for me to get here, but there is no man better suited for the job than Simon.

"Get a room already!" someone shouts.

"I reckon we should, don't you think?" Simon whispers against my lips. His hands drift down, pulling me closer to him.

"Later."

"Later? Christ, love, you and this later. You're going to drive a man mad. Haven't I suffered enough?"

I drag a finger along his lips, taking in every feature on his face. Memorizing it. "As long as I get all your laters, I'll make sure you won't suffer again."

"Later it is."

Chapter Thirty

SIMON

"You're the worst dancer I've ever seen!" Laughter bursts out of Layla as I do another crazy dance move.

"You know you love it." I smack a wet kiss on her cheek.

The party is in full swing. The minute the wedding ended, the reception began. Gemma and Blake didn't want anything fancy. No spotlight on them for the first dance. No cutting of the cake.

Just drinks, dancing, and all the cupcakes you could ever want.

Much to the excitement of all the kids at the wedding.

The song changes to a slower one and I pull the woman dancing with me into my arms.

"Care to dance with me, love?"

Layla beams up at me. "Show me what you've got, Belvy."

"You won't get rid of me if I'm a shite dancer, right?"

Wrapping her arms around me, she pulls me in close. The song playing is one I don't recognize.

"It would take a lot more than bad dancing to get rid of me."

I drop my forehead to hers. "Have I told you that I love you?"

Layla screws up her face in thought. "Not in the last hour or so."

"Need me to remind you again?"

She nods, biting on her lip.

"I love you, Layla."

"I love you, Simon." She steals a kiss from me. One that is too fucking short by my standards.

The night is still early. There's no telling when this will end, and I'm ready to bugger off because I want to spend every second with Layla.

We haven't given a single thought as to what happens next. We love each other. Before, we were just going to end this and no one would know differently.

Now? Now we need a plan on how to make this work. Being thousands of miles apart from Layla is too many. I don't want to be more than a room away from her right now.

I want the woman I love by my side.

"Can we go somewhere?" Layla whispers in my ear.

"Anything for you, love."

Linking her hand with mine, Layla and I walk out front, grabbing one of the waiting cars that Blake and Gemma arranged.

Layla rattles off an address to the driver. Her store.

Between the rehearsal and now, so much has happened that I barely processed the news when Pierce told me they actually closed her store.

Fucking Mrs. Bush.

I can't believe they would be so petty to close her store

because Layla doesn't fit their mold of what a store owner should be.

This woman is too good for this town.

The town is quiet as we pull up in front of her store. All the lights are off, only the streetlamps casting any sort of light into the shop.

Helping Layla out of the car, I can't help but notice how sad she looks. Tears gather in her eyes before she unlocks the door.

"Layla, I have to tell you something."

"What is it?"

"It's my fault that Brad found out."

"No." She shakes her head.

"It was. The night of the bachelor party. The guys kept firing questions at me and Pierce was being a wanker—"

"As he can be," she cuts in with a soft smile.

"And I snapped and told him. We were talking about it outside the bar and Brad bumped into me. He had to have heard me."

Layla shakes her head. "Whether he heard you or not, they were never going to let me keep this place."

"You're not mad?" I blow out a breath, taking her into my arms.

I don't know if he heard me or not, but this was something I had to tell Layla. It's the only logical explanation of how they found out. I still can't believe they bombarded her like this last night.

"I'm not. Did it bring the end of my store around faster? Yes. But if it brought me you, I'll never be upset about that."

"I love you." I kiss her tenderly. I love this woman so damn much, it's hard to breathe. "I am sorry. All I want to do is support you in this and I royally fucked up."

Layla smiles against my mouth. "You didn't."

Her eyes drift past me to the store.

"What's going through your head, love?" Layla takes everything in. Fingering the clothes still hanging from racks. Breathing in the smell of the store.

The smell that is all Layla. That beautiful orange and lavender scent.

"Pinstripes & Push-Ups has been my life for as long as I can remember. After my divorce, it's the only thing that kept me going."

"It doesn't have to end."

I follow Layla as she heads back to the dressing rooms. The Pinstripes & Push-Ups sign is backlit as she drops into one of the oversized chairs.

"I can't keep fighting this same fight with them."

Sweeping her into my arms, I sit in the chair with Layla on my lap.

"Then don't."

"What else am I supposed to do?"

"Come to London with me. Start a new business there?"

Layla pulls back, her eyes wide as she studies me. "But…"

I can see the retort written on her face before she says it. "Don't say your business is here. As sad as it is to say, it's not. You're meant for bigger things."

"Can I even move to London?"

I smile, tucking a stray lock of hair behind her ear. With the lights back here, Layla looks more beautiful than ever. Her hair is slightly out of place from dancing, and her makeup smudged, but I couldn't be more in love with this woman.

"I happen to know a certain princess who would likely be able to help with that."

"Is that allowed?" she laughs. "Can I bring Luna?"

"Of course we can bring Luna. I wouldn't leave that furball behind. We'll make it work. Hell, I know people that could help with the visa application."

"You want me to move to London with you?"

Layla chews on her lip, awaiting my answer. I pull her legs over so she's straddling me.

"I know your family is here, love, but you have family in London. People that love you there. Just because this place is closing doesn't mean you have to stop creating. Everything you make is beautiful. Why not share it with more people than just this small town?"

"Layla's of London. Kind of has a nice ring to it, no?"

"You'll come?"

Layla's fingers rub my jaw. "Was there ever any doubt? I want to be wherever you are."

"Christ, I love you."

I close the distance between us. Her mouth opens to mine at first contact. Each strike of her tongue against mine has me hardening in my pants.

Layla moans, shifting over me.

"I need you, Simon."

Best words I've ever heard.

"I'll give you whatever you need. Always."

Skilled fingers undo the zipper and belt on my pants. Her warm hand rubs over the growing bulge. "Fuck, does that ever feel good."

Layla's breath is hot over my mouth. I nibble on her lip, loving the whimper that escapes. My hands slide up and under her dress.

Warm skin is waiting for me.

"I don't know how much longer I can wait, Layla."

"Me either."

Grabbing my wallet, I pull out a condom and hand it

over to her. She pulls out my leaking dick and wastes no time sheathing me, lining herself up and sinking down.

"Fuck," I growl. "Fuck, Layla."

Her fingers dig into my shoulders, the bite of pain an even bigger turn-on.

"Simon."

Layla starts to move up and down. The erotic way she moves—the way she's taking what she wants—is fucking sexy as hell. Everything about her is.

"Faster, Layla."

My hands move up farther, guiding her hips. Each time she sinks down, I thrust up.

"I need you to come, love."

"So close."

Finding her clit, I strum my fingers over it. Sending her right over the edge.

"Simon!"

Her pussy squeezes my orgasm right out of me. I throw my head back, letting her take what she wants from me. For her? For her, I'd give her everything.

Layla slumps against me, breathing fast.

"That would be a first."

"A first for what?" I ask, curious as to where this is going.

"I guess a first and last. I've never done *that* in the store before."

Soft tendrils of hair curl around her face. "Maybe once you get your new store set up, we can break it in."

Layla's hazy eyes find mine. "It's going to be a lot of late nights. Getting some sort of store set up, you know that, right?"

"Maybe I can provide protection for you."

"Oh yeah?" She barks out a laugh. "I don't know if a lingerie shop owner is going to be a prime target."

"Mmm, no." I breathe her in. "But if it means I get to spend every night with you, then that's the lie I'll stick to."

"I can't wait to get to London."

Epilogue

SIMON · TEN MONTHS LATER

"You two are still coming, right?" I ask Pierce as I turn up the street.

"Relax, mate. We're putting the kids to bed, then we'll be over after most of the people leave. We wouldn't miss Layla's big night."

"Good. And our special guests are on their way?"

"Jesus, you're more worried than Layla."

"Fuck off."

"Maybe get a drink on the way over, yeah? You need to chill before you see Layla."

"I'm not nervous."

Except I am. I'll never tell Pierce or Layla that, but I'm anxious for her big night.

"Then you needed to call and remind me why?"

"I don't know why I'm friends with you."

"You love me."

"Yeah, yeah."

I hang up the phone, the small studio coming into view ahead of me. Slipping into the side door that leads to Layla's workspace, I'm met with a wall of noise.

Music is already blasting as caterers move about the space.

"What about the appetizers? Are they all out?" Layla spins on her heel, her long blonde hair flowing down her back. Pink colours her cheeks, likely from running around all day.

She looks fucking gorgeous tonight in one of her new pieces—a bralette with a cage framing around her breasts—with a slim blazer over the top and black pants. That skin showing on her stomach is tantalizing.

It has me shifting my hardening cock in my pants before making my presence known.

"Everything looks great, love."

Layla turns to face me, a beautiful smile playing on her lips.

"You're here."

"Where else would I be?" I wrap my arms around her waist, pulling her close to me. "Tonight's the night."

"What if something goes wrong?" Layla picks at the hem of my leather jacket.

Grasping her chin, I pull her blue eyes up to mine. No matter how nervous I am for her, I need to be her calming presence tonight. "You've got everything sorted out, yes?"

She nods.

"All the food and drinks?"

Another nod.

"And you've checked that everyone you've invited is coming?"

A final nod.

"Then stop worrying, love. Everything will go off without a hitch."

"But—"

I cut her off with a searing kiss to the lips. Even after

all these months, I still can't get over how good her lips feel against mine. How her body melds to every inch of mine.

I fucking love this woman and can't get enough of her.

I crave her more than the air I need to breathe.

"Is your plan to make me brainless tonight and not worry?" Layla's eyes are hazy as she pulls back from me.

"If it helps, then yes. Consider me on kissing duty tonight."

"How's that different from any other night?"

"Because," I growl, nipping at her lips, "I have to be on my best behaviour. I don't want you getting shut down on your first night because of indecent exposure."

Layla presses a quick kiss to my lips. "We'll just have to wait until we get home for that."

"And I can peel you out of this." I run my hands up her sides, feeling the fabric beneath my hands. Tracing the fine lines of the piece she's wearing.

"Hands to yourself until then." Layla removes my hands from her and takes a step back.

Even with the nerves evident, she looks ready.

For the last ten months, Layla has been building up her business here in London by selling her lingerie online. It wasn't easy starting her new company here. But with the help of the influencer she met last summer, she was able to make amazing headway and open her new store.

And now, everything she's worked so hard for is coming to fruition.

Her very own storefront in an up-and-coming fashion area in London.

Layla's. A change from the store in Dixon, but this is the fresh start she needed. I couldn't be more proud of all her hard work. Having a front row seat to everything she's built makes my chest swell with pride.

Each piece she created I saw firsthand. How it fit. The care behind it.

Not to mention how fucking gorgeous she looked in each of them.

Not that anyone needs to know that. That's our little secret.

"We're ready, Layla." Layla's newest assistant looks just as eager as she does.

"Okay." She runs both hands down the front of her blazer.

"You look stunning, love. Now go show everyone exactly what they need to buy tonight."

"I love you." She gives me another quick kiss and heads into the main shop.

I can't wait to see this woman in her element tonight. Because she deserves all of this and so much more.

Layla

My nerves have been getting the better of me all day. And now that the time is finally here?

I feel like they're ready to explode out of me.

Guests are already mingling as I look everything over from my spot at the back of the store.

Everything looks perfect. Pierce helped me find this coveted piece of real estate in Shoreditch on their main fashion street.

Exposed brick wall. High beams cutting across the ceiling. Vintage lights hanging from the ceiling. And a brand-new coat of bright white paint to make everything pop.

This store—Layla's—is a dream come true.

Not having to deal with the people in Dixon trying to put me down, I was able to create the perfect store. With help from Bri, my new favorite influencer, I was able to make this a reality.

Grabbing a glass of champagne from a passing server, I head into the crowd, stopping to talk with everyone. Telling them about my pieces and listening to their excitement.

It's a blur, really. This whole night. People come and go, but Simon has taken up residence on the fringes of the store, keeping an ever watchful eye on everything. Ever the protector.

It's then I notice who he's talking to.

"If you'll excuse me a moment." I smile at the couple I've been chatting with and make a beeline for a face I've missed more than I realized.

"Gemma! What are you doing here?"

"Surprise!"

I pull her in for a tight hug, tears prickling my eyes.

"I talked to you last night and you were at home."

I can't believe my little sister is in London right now.

"You didn't think we'd miss your big night, did you?"

"But how?"

Blake is standing behind her, talking with Simon. Even with how little we make it back to Dixon, those two are as thick as thieves.

"We flew in yesterday. Layla,"—Gemma's eyes fill with tears—"this is incredible. I am so proud of you."

She pulls me in for another hug, my emotions now getting the best of me.

I've been working for so long at this, it's hard to believe that it's real. That these beautiful creations I made—made to make people feel beautiful and empowered—are real. It's a shift from Pinstripes & Push-Ups. No more clothes. Just lingerie.

And now I even have a team helping me design and create.

"How long are you here for?" I ask.

"Another week. Shooting doesn't start back up for a few weeks, so we're taking a real vacation."

"Hey!" Blake cuts in. "I've taken you on plenty of vacations this year."

"Yes, but something always comes up and you end up having to work a few of those days."

"Okay, not entirely untrue. But it's not like issues haven't come up at the ranch either."

Being around Blake and Gemma makes me realize how much I miss home.

London has done nothing but welcome me with open arms, but it was harder to adjust to life in the big city than I thought.

But I wouldn't trade what Simon and I have for anything.

A small apartment overlooking a quiet square. An interfering cat.

And family close by that have been there for me every minute I've needed them this year.

"We're going to go peruse everything you've made. I can't wait to see it up close." Gemma's eyes are twinkling as she reaches back for Blake.

I don't miss their heated stares at one another.

"If you buy anything, I don't want to know," I shout at their retreating backs as they head into the crowd of people.

"What other surprises do you have for me, Mr. Belvy?"

I wrap my arms around Simon, knowing he had everything to do with this. His strong muscles flex as he envelops me in his hold.

"It wouldn't be a surprise, now would it, Miss Winchester, if I told you?"

"Surprise or no surprise, I don't think this night could get any better."

"I take it everyone is loving it?"

I nod, at a loss for words.

Simon's strong hand clasps my cheek. Warmth seeps into me.

I love this man more than I ever thought possible.

"I knew they would. How could anyone not see how bloody brilliant everything you've created is?'

This man's faith in me has been unwavering. I'd be nowhere without his support.

"I keep waiting for something to go wrong and it hasn't. I can't believe what a success this has been."

"It's only the beginning, love."

Beginning of everything with this man. I can't wait for everything that is to come. With him by my side, I know we can take on anything.

Because the love we have is more real than anything else I've ever experienced.

Thank God for my fake fiancé.

The End

Want to read more about those royals? Then be sure to check out my Ainsworth Royals series now, starting with Royal Reckoning…

Read on for another bonus scene with Layla and Simon…

Bonus Scene

LAYLA

"You want to go out for drinks?" Gemma drops her head on my shoulder. "We need to celebrate tonight."

"Aren't you exhausted?" I lay my head on hers. I still can't believe she's here.

Tonight was everything I wanted and more. Having some of my favorite people here to celebrate my new store opening made the night even better.

"No. We've only got so much time here and I'm not going to waste it sleeping."

"Why don't we meet you guys at the pub?" Blake elbows Simon in the side. The two of them share a look.

"Are the pubs still open?" Gemma asks.

"We know a place," Pierce chimes in. "Take your time."

"Thank you all for coming tonight." I get choked up. "I really can't believe you're here and that this is happening."

"Believe it." Charlotte pulls me into a hug. "I'm so proud of you."

I give her and everyone else around me hugs as they

start to leave the store. Remnants from the evening are scattered around. Simon grabs me before I can start to do any cleaning.

"It can wait until tomorrow, love."

Emotions overwhelm me as I take in my empty store. I never imagined tonight would've gone this well. Call me tentative because of how things ended back home, but tears threaten to spill over at how perfect it went.

"What are you thinking?" Simon wraps his arms around me.

"I never thought I'd get this."

"You're incredible." Simon presses a warm kiss to my neck. "You deserve all the good things in the world, love."

"As long as I have you, I'll have all the good things in the world."

"C'mon. Let's go meet them for drinks."

I sink into Simon's hold. "Thank you, Simon."

"I'm always here for you. No matter what."

I don't know how I got so lucky to find this man. I've never felt more love or support from someone in my life. Sure, my family has always been there, but Simon? It takes my breath away with having him by my side.

"Let's go."

Simon links his hand with mine. Any mess in here can wait until tomorrow. The official opening is in a few days. I know I'll be a basketcase up until then, but tonight?

Tonight I want to enjoy Simon and spend time with my family.

Our walk is slow as Simon has a place in mind.

"Where are we going?"

"It's a surprise." Simon slips his hand under my blazer, his big hand warm against my back, steering me down another side street.

"You know how I feel about surprises."

"I promise, love," he whispers against my temple, "you'll like it."

"Fine." There's no real argument in my voice. I'd go anywhere Simon takes me.

Like London. Never in my wildest dreams did I think I'd be living here. I thought Dixon was it for me. That I'd grow old by myself and Luna.

Simon has given me more than I could have wished for. It's like all my dreams are coming true.

Pubs are overflowing with people on the sidewalks as we pass. I love how no matter what time it is, the city is always buzzing with energy.

It took me some time to adapt to life here, but now, I can't imagine being anywhere else.

"What are we doing here?"

Simon stops in front of St. Dunstan's. It's after ten. It's long since closed.

"You'll see."

"Are we allowed to be here?" I whisper as he unlocks the gate.

"I have the keys, don't I?" Simon quirks his lips at me.

"I guess so."

As the old gate creaks open, the inside of the park comes to life in front of my eyes.

"Simon."

"C'mon, love."

Simon grabs my hand, pulling me inside. The old, bombed-out church looks nothing like it normally does. Old vines cover the sides of the church, but now? Now hundreds of tiny candles line the ground.

My heart catches in my throat as I drink everything in around me.

This was one of the first places Simon brought me when I got here. It's special. We haven't been here as often as I'd like with the store opening, but tonight will more than make up for it.

Spinning on my heel, Simon is walking toward me.

Simon pulls me into his arms, holding me like we have all the time in the world. I breathe him in. This moment. I want to commit everything about this night to memory.

"I've got something I want to ask you, love," Simon whispers into my ear. It has butterflies erupting in my stomach.

"Oh yeah?"

Pulling away, Simon drops down onto one knee. His eyes are glowing amongst the candles. He reaches into his pocket and pulls out a black, velvet box.

The silver, solitaire engagement ring is stunning.

"Layla. Everything about our love story has been unconventional. I never thought that I'd find you when I went to Dixon. Let alone become your fake boyfriend and then fake fiancé in the span of a day. Every moment since has been the best adventure. I'll never get tired of making you laugh. Of watching the way your face lights up when you design some new piece that will blow everyone away. You are the most talented, beautiful, kind and caring person I've ever met."

Tears are running down my face as Simon takes a breath.

"Will you make me the happiest man alive and do me the honor of becoming my wife?"

"Yes!" I tackle him to the ground, landing on the–*thank-fully*–plastic candles. "Yes!"

I pepper his face with kisses, not a breath of air coming between our bodies.

"Want me to get this ring on?" Simon asks against my mouth.

"Uh huh." My fingers trace over his face, not believing this moment is happening.

Simon slides the ring on my ring. The diamond catches the light around us as I stare down at it.

It's perfect.

I never thought I'd want to get married again. Been there, done that.

Turns out, I was just waiting for the right person.

"It's gorgeous."

"It belonged to my grandmum."

"I love it." I press another kiss to his warm lips. I love that I have something so special to him. "I love you."

It's quiet here. Like our own oasis in the middle of London. This place is mostly bypassed by tourists, which makes me love it even more.

"I love you, Layla. I'm glad you're finally mine."

"I've always been yours, Simon."

He shakes his head. "Finally my real fiancée. No more fake."

I drag my nose along his. "Real fiancé. Sounds pretty nice."

The best words I've ever spoken.

I can't believe I get to marry this man I love more than anything in the world.

"Best real fiancé indeed."

Author's Note

Book 15 is out in the world!

One of my favorite things about this book is combining so many of my worlds…the Ainsworth Royals, Dixon and the Mountain Lions! I've loved dropping in on some of my favorite couples while writing Simon and Layla's story. These two are one of my favorite couples (shh! Don't tell the others!) and I am so thankful you picked up Yours To Be!

I have been so blessed to have so many amazing author friends that have been with me on this journey. Swati, Lily, Claire, Suzanne, Maria, Stephanie, Jodi…I love all of you so much and thank you for keeping me sane! To Tina… one of my favorite people in the book world..I love you!

Thank you to my beta readers Jodi and Ashlee for making this book amazing! I'm so happy to have you on this journey with me. Thank you to every person that has read, reviewed, shared, created edits, TikToked…you name it, your support has been the best part of this journey. To my Street Team for your excitement for my books always puts a smile on my face! And my Travelers…my group is my favorite little corner of the internet!

And to all the readers…I hope you love this new world I've built as much as I do! Your support means the world to me!

<3 Emily

About the Author

After winning a Young Author's Award in second grade, Emily Silver was destined to be a writer. She loves writing strong heroines and the swoony men who fall for them.

A lover of all things romance, Emily started writing books set in her favorite places around the world. As an avid traveler, she's been to all seven continents and sailed around the globe.

When she's not writing, Emily can be found sipping cocktails on her porch, reading all the romance she can get her hands on and planning her next big adventure!

Find her on social media to stay up to date on all her adventures and upcoming releases!

Also by Emily Silver

Dixon Creek Ranch

Yours to Take

Yours to Hold

Yours to Be

Yours to Forget - coming winter, 2023

The Denver Mountain Lions

Roughing The Kicker

Pass Interference

Sideline Infraction

Illegal Contact

The Big Game

Off the Deep End — A standalone, MM sports romance

The Ainsworth Royals

Royal Reckoning

Reckless Royal

Royal Relations

Royal Roots

Royal Ties

The Love Abroad Series

An Icy Infatuation

A French Fling

A Sydney Surprise

Get the trope guide on my website, or

scan the QR code to read all my books on Kindle Unlimited

www.ingramcontent.com/pod-product-compliance
Lightning Source LLC
Chambersburg PA
CBHW021309190726
48288CB00003B/754